# RIGHT CAN BE WRONG

*Right Can Be Wrong*
Copyright © 2024 Cary Hendrix Jr.

All rights reserved. No part of this book may be reproduced (except for inclusion in reviews), disseminated or utilized in any form or by any means, electronic or mechanical, including photocopying, recording, or in any information storage and retrieval system, or the Internet/World Wide Web without written permission from the author or publisher.

Printed in the United States of America

*Right Can Be Wrong*
Cary Hendrix Jr.

ISBN 13: 979-8-8786-8823-9

Also By CARY HENDRIX JR.

NOTES OF A NOBODY

THINGS 'N' GENERAL

IN BLACK AND WHITE

To All Those PEOPLE WHO Are STRUGGLING To Be THEMSELVES.

"THERE IS NOTHING EITHER GOOD or BAD,
BUT THINKING MAKES IT SO."

WILLIAM SHAKESPEARE

Raising children is MOSTLY A JOY or MOSTLY A CHALLENGE.

Raising children is a challenge for some, because WE accept THE JOB, before WE have learned "THE SKILL."

RAISING CHILDREN is "THE ART" that FEW PARENTS STUDY.

Much of our EDUCATION SYSTEM teaches OUR CHILDREN some subjects that will not DIRECTLY AFFECT THEM, and does not TEACH some subjects that will, such as teaching CHILDCARE and MONEY MANAGEMENT to older adolescents.

UNLIKE FARMERS, we are ALLOWED to PRODUCE CHILDREN, before WE HAVE LEARNED HOW TO GROW THEM.

Our BODIES MATURE before WE DO.

Our PUBLIC LIVES are not our REAL LIVES; our real lives are our PRIVATE LIVES.

Some FANS DO NOT KNOW their private lives ARE HAPPIER than the private lives of THE CELEBRITIES that they IDOLIZE or ADMIRE.

Those "ON THE BOTTOM" tend to try TO BRING THINGS DOWN TO THEIR LEVEL.

We cannot see THE DARKNESS of POP CULTURE, because it is COVERED WITH GLITTER.

If MOVING HIGHER is TOO DIFFICULT, we may SETTLE for something LOWDOWN.

If we PRAISE OURSELVES with our thoughts, it may be SELF-CONFIDENCE; but if we praise ourselves to others, it is more likely to be ARROGANCE or CONCEIT.

Some of us GO TOO FAR, because we don't KNOW HOW FAR, "TOO FAR" IS.

ALL EXTREMES are HAZARDOUS.

We use the words "HELP" and "ASSIST" interchangeably; we can better ASSIST PEOPLE than we can "HELP THEM."

We cannot spiritually HELP or SAVE PEOPLE; we can only ASSIST THEM in spiritually HELPING or SAVING THEMSELVES.

SCIENCE is what we KNOW; RELIGION is what we BELIEVE.

GOD and LOVE are WHATEVER most of us WANT THEM TO BE.

If "THERE IS A TIME, A REASON, AND SEASON FOR EVERYTHING," we do not always KNOW THE TIME, THE REASON or THE SEASON.

There are SO MANY "SIDES" to GOD, LOVE and LIFE; but we ONLY WANT THEM TO BE SEEN FROM "OUR SIDE."

EVERYONE can NEVER BE ON OUR SIDE.

We cannot LIVE TOO LONG, but WE CAN LIVE TOO WRONG.

We cannot "FIX" everyone WHO IS BROKEN.

How our children TURN-OUT is not ALWAYS COMMENSURATE with HOW THEY WERE RAISED.

Some celebrities who are WELL KNOWN, are not KNOWN WELL.

New GUN LAWS will only DEPRIVE LAW ABIDERS of GUNS.

"GUNS DON'T KILL PEOPLE," PEOPLE with GUNS KILL PEOPLE.

Some of America's POOR would be MIDDLE-CLASS in some THIRD WORLD countries.

America's FOUNDING FATHERS fled OPPRESSION in EUROPE, to come to THE NEW WORLD, to OPPRESS BLACK AFRICANS.

"ALL LIVES WILL NOT MATTER," until BLACK or MINORITY LIVES MATTER TOO.

Our GREATEST FRIEND and ENEMY is OURSELVES.

Some BLACK and WHITE people are only SEPARATED by A SINGLE WORD.

The kind of LIFE we are living "NOW," is because of what we did or did not do "THEN."

Taking "THE EASY WAY," will ultimately TURN OUT to have been THE WRONG or WORST WAY.

The BESTSELLING PRODUCT sold in AMERICA is "MONEY."

Some BLACK PEOPLE HATE SNOW, because IT LOOKS too much LIKE COTTON.

Initially, IN AMERICA, we CAN BUY almost anything we wish – WITHOUT MONEY.

The "TAKERS" never GIVE, and "THE GIVERS" are more likely to GET TAKEN.

The better way to find some things is to NOT LOOK FOR THEM.

Some of us TRY TO LIFT OURSELVES UP by PUTTING PEOPLE DOWN.

We cannot FIGHT LIFE'S BATTLES, without BEING HURT or "WOUNDED."

LAUGHTER is to keep us from becoming TOO SERIOUS, and SERIOUSNESS is to keep us from becoming TOO SILLY.

It is so difficult to "PRACTICE WHAT WE PREACH," because nearly everything is "EASIER SAID THAN DONE."

NUMBERS are the only things in LIFE that are "AVERAGE."

Some people ARE RIGHT who are NOT EXPERTS, and some people ARE WRONG who ARE EXPERTS.

IF THE LAWS are not ALWAYS RIGHT, then LAWBREAKERS are not ALWAYS WRONG.

Can a WHITE PERSON dislike a BLACK PERSON without it being PREJUDICE or RACISM?

Some ROMANTICS who are searching FOR "THE RIGHT ONE," may not know "THEY ARE THE WRONG ONE."

We do not NEED TO MOSTLY CHANGE OTHERS; we need to MOSTLY CHANGE OURSELVES.

The people most difficult TO SEE CLEARLY are THOSE CLOSEST TO US.

ROMANTIC RELATIONSHIPS are "NOT OVER 'TIL THEY'RE OVER."

RIGHT CAN BE WRONG

MOST PEOPLE cannot tell us what they would do IF THEY HAD OUR PROBLEM, unless THEY HAVE HAD OUR PROBLEM.

THE BETTER romantic relationship is probably A GOOD MARRIAGE, and probably THE WORST, is A BAD MARRIAGE.

The LAST PERSON most of us will BLAME for anything, is OURSELVES.

HISTORICALLY or TRADITIONALLY, we have always USED GOD as AN EXCUSE or EXPLANATION for all our IGNORANCE.

The people who ARE BEST FOR THE JOB are not always THE PEOPLE WE LIKE.

Not All GOOD ACTORS are STARS, and NOT ALL STARS are GOOD ACTORS.

We do not ALWAYS need to know WHERE WE CAME FROM, to know WHERE WE WANT TO GO.

It is difficult for THE ELDERLY to talk to THE YOUNG, because elderly people HAVE A PAST, but young people DO NOT.

The WORST THING we can do for SOME INDIVIDUAL POLICE OFFICERS, is TO GIVE THEM A GUN.

Never GET INVOLVED in A FIGHT, unless you can "TAKE A PUNCH."

If we WRITE A BOOK OF NONSENSE and a lot of people BUY IT, our BOOK OF NONSENSE will become "A BEST SELLER."

Some RELATIVES pretend to be our FRIENDS, and some FRIENDS, we wish were our RELATIVES.

Can MOST YOUNG PEOPLE getting MARRIED make promises to last for THE REST OF THEIR LIVES?

WEAK PEOPLE are ALWAYS TELLING US HOW STRONG THEY ARE; STRONG PEOPLE SHOW US.

We want to KNOW other PEOPLE'S BUSINESS, but OUR OWN BUSINESS is "PRIVATE."

We are "HUMAN-ANIMALS," and some of us are MORE ANIMAL THAN HUMAN.

The ULTIMATE GOAL of HUMAN-ANIMALS is to be MORE HUMAN and LESS OF AN ANIMAL.

CELEBRITIES are rarely who THEY SAY THEY ARE, or who WE THINK THEY ARE.

In America, RELIGION is as much "A BUSINESS" as FORD and GM.

In America, we are all trying to OUT-SPEAK or OUT-DO one another, before "ALL IS SAID AND DONE."

Almost everything we do on "THE OUTSIDE" began on "THE INSIDE."

Whenever WE TRY TO FIND SOMETHING IMPORTANT, it will BE HARD TO FIND.

When we are LOOKING FOR SOMETHING, we LOST TODAY we will only FIND WHAT WE LOST YESTERDAY.

People WHO WON'T LISTEN TO US, expect US TO LISTEN TO THEM.

MOST SEXUAL RELATIONSHIPS function by DIFFERENT RULES than MOSTLY LOVING RELATIONSHIPS.

ALAS, in present day AMERICA, A WHITE PERSON can get to "THE TOP" without THE ASSISTANCE of A BLACK PERSON, much easier than A BLACK PERSON can get there without THE ASSISTANCE OF A WHITE PERSON.

It HURTS OUR FEELINGS, when people WON'T THINK WHAT WE THINK or BELIEVE WHAT WE BELIEVE.

DUMB PEOPLE tend TO THINK THEY ARE SMART, and SMART PEOPLE KNOW HOW DUMB THEY ARE.

SOMEONE will always TRY TO GET RICH, from GOVERNMENT PROGRAMS to ASSIST THE POOR.

PEOPLE WHO DO NOT KNOW "WHO THEY ARE," tend to THINK THEY ARE SOMEONE ELSE.

We REVERE people who are SAINTLY and FEAR people who are EVIL.

In AMERICA, EVERYONE with an opinion, USUALLY, has A RIGHT to be WRONG.

SOME of our FAULTS and FLAWS can be TRACED BACK to LESSONS "NOT LEARNED" in our EARLY NURTURING.

POVERTY in AMERICA is not "A MONEY PROBLEM," it is A SPIRITUAL PROBLEM.

We are NOT HELPING POOR PEOPLE, by GIVING THEM MONEY or NICE THINGS. The only way to HELP is to ASSIST THEM in finding THE WHEREWITHAL to HELP THEMSELVES.

## RIGHT CAN BE WRONG

Without MEANS or PRIOR PREPARATIONS, FREEDOM for SLAVES, were both "A BLESSING" and "A CURSE."

Can "AN ATHEIST" be LOVING, and "A BELIEVER be DEVILISH?"

Some people who ARE THE PROBLEM believe they are THE SOLUTION.

Which is BETTER or WORST: AN HONEST ATHEIST or A DISHONEST BELIEVER?

We SURVIVE by RATIONALIZING or JUSTIFYING our FAULTS and FLAWS.

A SUDDEN WINDFALL can be an INSTANT DOWNFALL for some people.

Not every "ADULT" is AN ADULT.

Neither GOOD nor BAD things END; They move in A CYCLE.

Some of us DO NOT FIND LOVE; LOVE FINDS US.

A MAJOR PROBLEM can make us forget about A MINOR ONE.

We do not have to BE ALONE to be LONELY; the SADDEST LONELINESS is when we are in a family, a relationship or a group.

Some TALENTED PEOPLE are NOT FAMOUS and SOME FAMOUS PEOPLE are NOT TALENTED.

If only WHITE PEOPLE determine what BLACK HISTORY IS, it will be TEPID or LUKEWARM; if BLACK PEOPLE mostly determine what is their HISTORY, it will be TOO INTENSE for many WHITE PEOPLE to tolerate.

The VARIOUS HUES OF COLOR in "BLACK PEOPLE" represent A TREMENDOUS VIOLATION of AN ENTIRE PEOPLE.

LEGALIZED GAMBLING OFFERS US "HEAVEN," but MOSTLY GIVES US "HELL."

All of us do not worship in a TRADITIONAL RELIGION, but nearly ALL OF US "WORSHIP MONEY."

Since WE ALL "WORSHIP MONEY," those who have THE MOST are generally DEEMED TO BE "THE BEST PEOPLE."

MONEY is our "SECULAR GOD," because IT INFLUENCES or CONTROLS ALMOST EVERYTHING.

IF MONEY IS NOT "EVERYTHING," is ANYTHING, EVERYTHING?

When most people say that someone has "A LARGE EGO," they really mean that they have "A SMALL EGO," or SENSE OF SELF. A person with a GENUINELY LARGE EGO does not require a lot of STROKING or PRAISE.

CELEBRITIES will only support what is POPULAR, PROFITABLE and WHAT MAKES THEM "LOOK GOOD."

The first thing THAT IS KILLED in "A WAR," is LOVE, LOGIC, REASON and JUSTICE.

It is ABSOLUTELY TRUE that few things are ABSOLUTELY TRUE.

SOME of us will try to GET AWAY WITH, as much as we are ALLOWED TO GET WAY WITH.

If ENOUGH PEOPLE do not THINK YOU ARE RIGHT, they will OPPOSE YOUR RIGHT TO BE WRONG.

Do you think or believe that the further we look in THE PAST, the less we can rely on what we SEE?

PROSTITUTION exists in MANY FORMS, including in some MARRIAGES and THE RELATIONSHIP between "GOLD DIGGERS" and "SUGAR DADDIES."

MOST OF AMERICAN LIFE is STRUCTURED in favor of THE RICH, THE FAMOUS, THE POWERFUL and "THE WHITES."

We are willing to QUESTION, INSPECT or EXAMINE everyone, EXCEPT OURSELVES.

Some "FREE SPEECH" can be VERY COSTLY.

YOU cannot GIVE ADVICE to someone who has A GREATER DESIRE to GIVE ADVICE TO YOU.

The MOST DIFFICULT PERSON to SEE CLEARLY is OURSELVES.

We are AFRAID of BEING AFRAID, but we are not SCARED of BEING SCARED.

THE HARDEST THINGS for us TO FACE in LIFE – IS DEATH.

Some MARRIAGES become BETTER, after they SURVIVE the WORSE.

SOME POLICE OFFICERS are "LEGALIZED BULLIES," and THEY FEEL that anyone WHO RESISTS or OPPOSES them IN THE STREETS, are "THE ENEMY."

*RIGHT CAN BE WRONG*

We can FEEL BADLY because we have "NOTHING," and we can FEEL BADLY because we have "EVERYTHING."

Some people believe that the QUICKEST WAY to LOSE WEIGHT, is TO FAST.

It is too easy for us to PAT OURSELVES ON THE BACK and too difficult for us TO ACCEPT BLAME.

Some RELIGIOUS PEOPLE will verbally CONDEMN OTHERS TO "HELL AND DAMNATION," then CLAIM THAT THEY HAVE FORGIVEN THEM.

Some POLITICIANS are SO SLY or CUNNING, that some PEOPLE think THEY ARE SMART or CLEVER.

NEW TRUTHS tend to UPSET, FRIGHTEN or ANGER US.

We have chosen to ENVY the PEOPLE we perceive to be ABOVE US, rather than BE HAPPY we are not the people we perceive to be BELOW US.

"GIVERS" want to be around us when it is BENEFICIAL TO US, but "TAKERS" only want to be around us when it is BENEFICIAL TO THEM.

It is THE FAULTS, FLAWS, PROBLEMS and DIFFERENCES between people that MAKES LIFE INTERESTING; if we were all "PERFECT," LIFE WOULD BE BORING.

Which do you think is MORE SIGNIFICANT: How WE TREAT LIFE or HOW LIFE TREATS US?

Some CHILDREN will not SEE how SILLY they once were, until THEY ARE PARENTS.

CAPITAL PUNISHMENT is such an ill-advised "punishment" because it allows heinous criminals to escape being sentient of their punishment and relegates them to the same FATE as everyone else. It only satisfies our own personal sense of vengeance, it does nothing against the accused; in fact, some troubled people VOLUNTEER for it.

CAPITAL PUNISHMENT is not for "THEM"; it is only for US.

We are not IMPRESSIVE PEOPLE unless IMPRESSIVE PEOPLE think WE ARE IMPRESSIVE.

IMPRESSIVE PEOPLE are the HARDEST PEOPLE to IMPRESS.

The BETTER WAY TO IMPRESS is to IMPRESS, without TRYING to IMPRESS.

It is difficult for THE RICH, FAMOUS and POWERFUL people to NOT THINK that they are "SOMETHING SPECIAL," rather than VERY FORTUNATE.

LIFE always ENDS before WE HAVE FINISHED LIVING IT.

Do you ever read BIBLICAL LORE and PONDER, why GOD had A SON and not A DAUGHTER?

So WHY would THE HOLY BOOKS be CONFORMING to ANCIENT "SEXIST" NORMS?

RELIGIOUS PROSELYTIZERS never think they are IMPOSING, because they think they know WHAT IS BEST FOR US, better THAN WE DO.

Do you think THE INSIGNIFICANCE of WOMEN in THE HOLY BOOKS is indicative OF GOD or THE SEXIST MEN who wrote THE HOLY BOOKS?

STUPID, FOOLISH, IGNORANT or WEAK PEOPLE like their POLITICIANS that way too.

All EARTHLY "DEVILS" hide behind and DEFEND THEMSELVES with HOLY SCRIPTURE.

The difference between A STRONG SPIRITUAL LEADER and A COMMON CRIMINAL is that the STRONG SPIRITUAL LEADER is WILLING to go to jail.

Some people must make others FEEL LIKE NOTHING, for them to FEEL LIKE SOMETHING.

We can SOLVE SOME PROBLEMS, some PROBLEMS we CANNOT SOLVE, and SOME PROBLEMS SOLVE THEMSELVES.

Whatever YOU THINK IS VERY SACRED or VERY SERIOUS in LIFE, someone thinks IT IS A JOKE.

Do you THINK that GOD EXISTS more FIGURATIVELY than LITERALLY?

We FALLIBLE HUMANS have great difficulty SEPARATING THE FIGURATIVE from THE LITERAL.

ALL LIFE is LIVED in DENIAL of DEATH.

After we have expressed our COMPASSION or SYMPATHY to those who have experienced A TRAGEDY, we feel happy that IT DID NOT HAPPEN TO US.

Do you believe in "AN AFTER LIFE," or do you believe that the word DEAD means DEAD?

*RIGHT CAN BE WRONG*

Elderly people can "SEE" farther down "LIFE'S ROAD" than YOUNG PEOPLE, so young people cannot see what they are TRYING TO POINT OUT TO THEM.

If we LEARN from OUR FAILURES, and are BLESSED by OUR SUCCESSES, then "IT IS ALL GOOD."

Why weren't things like SLAVERY and CHILD MOLESTATION mentioned in THE TEN COMMANDMENTS?

Our lives are MOSTLY JOYFUL, FULL OF CHALLENGES or OUT OF CONTROL.

We all know "WHAT WE ARE," but THE WORLD will not always allow us to be "WHO WE ARE."

CELEBRITIES are CELEBRATED for being GOOD or BAD.

There is no definitive definition for GOD or LOVE that we all can agree with; but we all think we understand what people mean whenever they speak about them. Sometimes, we are NOT TALKING ABOUT THE SAME THINGS.

Do you BELIEVE or THINK that SOME PEOPLE start "NON-PROFITS" to MAKE A PROFIT?

In PAST POPULAR ADVENTURE STORIES, WHY Is "THE KING OF THE JUNGLE," always A WHITE MAN?

We can only order PHYSICAL THINGS "ONLINE"; we cannot order LOVE, PEACE, HAPPINESS or SPIRITUAL THINGS.

FEELINGS and EMOTIONS get in the way of OUR LOGIC and REASONING.

We cannot believe everything people say ABOUT THEMSELVES, because people do not always KNOW THEMSELVES

Some words FEEL and SOUND just like their MEANINGS: words like SLICE, SLEAZY, OILY, SLICK, GREASY and ICY.

There are some words we cannot FEEL, and some FEELINGS we cannot PUT INTO WORDS.

Some people who want CREDIT for SAVING THE WORLD, cannot SAVE THEMSELVES.

Do we HAVE "A RIGHT to OUR FEELINGS," if our FEELINGS are not "RIGHT?"

Do we have "A RIGHT" to HATE?

Is "FREEDOM OF SPEECH," ABSOLUTE?

Sometimes, things THAT ARE WRONG, are STILL ALL RIGHT.

When we say, "LIFE IS SHORT" – COMPARED TO WHAT?

Perhaps it would behoove us to stop "LOVING PEOPLE TO DEATH" and START LOVING PEOPLE "TO LIFE."

Is there anything better than A GREAT FRIENDSHIP, as the foundation for A STRONG MARRIAGE?

SOME RELIGIONS get some people TO JOIN THEM by making them AFRAID NOT TO.

Is our RELIGIOSITY mostly FAITH or FEAR?

Do WHITE PEOPLE ever PONDER why "ANGRY BLACK PEOPLE" are SO ANGRY?

We do not just want to be BIG, BETTER, HAPPY or GREAT; we want to be THE BIGGEST, THE BEST, THE HAPPIEST and THE GREATEST.

Do you ever wonder what kind of country AMERICA would have become, WERE IT NOT FOR SLAVERY?

Most women will not VOLUNTEER their age, unless they feel that they LOOK MUCH YOUNGER.

Since it is NOT POSSIBLE to CORROBORATE or VALIDATE, we can claim THAT GOD HAS TOLD US ANYTHING WE WISH.

True SAINTS do not speak or brag about their RIGHTEOUSNESS; THEY DEMONSTRATE IT.

Most RELIGIOUS PEOPLE are "ALL PREACH" and LITTLE PRACTICE.

The CURIOSITY of small children is so INTENSE that there is nothing we can hide from them INSIDE OUR HOUSE, especially OUR GUNS.

Some WOMEN CONDEMN their female friends for INFIDELITY; some MEN APPLAUD their male friends for it.

POOR PEOPLE pay more FOR EVERYTHING than everyone else, RELATIVELY SPEAKING.

The ONLY THING that some people within A RACE or ETHNICITY have IN COMMON, is THEIR RACE and ETHNICITY.

YOUNG PEOPLE don't always know WHERE THEY ARE GOING, and ELDERLY PEOPLE tend to want to return to WHERE THEY CAME FROM.

*RIGHT CAN BE WRONG*

Once we become "AN IDOL" we can no longer BE A HUMAN.

Most of us are more apt to GIVE ADVICE than TAKE IT.

We are ALL INDIVIDUAL combinations of GOOD, BAD, TRUTH and LIES.

We tend to RATIONALIZE or MANIPULATE our RELIGIOSITY to support what we like, and to CONDEMN what we dislike.

We are ALL "IMPERFECT," and we all go through life BLAMING ONE ANOTHER FOR IT.

EVOLUTION is CHANGE that WE KNOW but CANNOT SEE.

EVOLUTION is something like WATCHING THE GRASS GROW, we know it is happening, but we can never SEE or CATCH THE GRASS MOVING.

For some of us, PARENTING is "ON THE JOB TRAINING."

Can WE claim TO BE "SPIRITUAL" while WE are OBSESSED with OUR "PHYSICAL" APPEARANCE?

GOD probably wants us to be CARING, LOVING, SENSITIVE or KIND, but probably DOES NOT CARE HOW WE LOOK.

It is very difficult to eliminate NEPOTISM, because all of us WANT TO HELP OUR OWN.

Sometimes, THE BEST PERSON to be PRESIDENT or LEADER, is the person WHO DOES NOT WANT TO BE THE PRESIDENT or LEADER.

Some INTELLECTUALS are VERY DEEP, and some ARE JUST "OVER-THINKING."

FAME is SO ESTEEMED, because THE MORE PEOPLE WHO LIKE US, the more WE TEND TO LIKE OURSELVES.

Don't CELEBRITIES have ENOUGH AWARD SHOWS; how much "PRAISE" or "STROKING" do they NEED?

There is always something to GET OVER, GET THROUGH or LEARN TO TOLERATE.

It is difficult to be "SATISFIED," The moment we get what we wanted, we start wanting what we could not get.

We want to know about HOW MUCH others are worth, but don't want others TO KNOW WHAT WE ARE WORTH.

SUDDEN WEALTH does not always CHANGE US, but always changes "THEM."

SLAVERY ONCE was thought to be RIGHT; but NOW, EVERYONE except RACISTS, thinks that it was WRONG.

OUR WORDS tend to REVEAL WHAT WE THINK, but OUR FACES REVEAL what WE FEEL.

If we want to LESSEN OUR "PROBLEMS" we should never get involved WITH OTHER PEOPLE. If we want to lessen OUR LOVE, JOY and HAPPINESS, we should never get involved WITH OTHER PEOPLE.

Some MOTHERS DO NOT WANT TO RAISE A PERSON; they want to just POSSESS someone CUTE AND CUDDLY.

When people say someone "HAS CHANGED THE WORLD," they usually mean only A SMALL PART OF IT.

"HOLY WAR" is A MISNOMER

People who can LOOK beyond OUR LOOKS, can SEE OUR SPIRITS.

SHORT ROMANCES are MOSTLY BASED on LOOKS; LONG ROMANCES are MOSTLY BASED on SPIRITS.

We say, "I LOVE YOU" so much, that we are NOT likely TO MEAN IT every time WE SAY IT.

Do you MOSTLY CONTROL your LIFE, or DOES YOUR LIFE mostly CONTROL YOU?

PRAYER is GOOD FOR THE PRAY-ER.

NOTHING IS "GOOD FOR NOTHING."

SLAVES IN AMERICA were never allowed to ESTABLISH A FAMILY LIFE, because children were SOLD from the breasts of their mothers. And MOST OF TODAY'S RACISTS enjoy complaining about how BLACK FAMILY LIFE is UNSTABLE.

If we are 'THINKING" while SITTING STILL, we are NOT "DOING NOTHING."

BLOOD may be "THICKER than WATER," but LOVE is "THICKER" than BLOOD.

In "THE LAND OF THE BLIND," it is "THE SIGHTED PEOPLE" who are HANDICAPPED.

Some WOMEN do not KNOW what they are PHYSICALLY CAPABLE OF, unless there are NO MEN NEARBY.

Most BLACK PEOPLE over SIXTY YEARS of Age, have at least ONE PICTURE in their home of JESUS CHRIST, JOHN F.

*RIGHT CAN BE WRONG*

KENNEDY, NELSON MANDELA, MARTIN LUTHER KING JR. or BARACK OBAMA or ALL OF THE ABOVE.

Do you ever wonder HOW MUCH POLICE CORRUPTION EXISTED before police WERE FORCED to WEAR BODY CAMS?

SCRIPTURE says that there was A WAR in HEAVEN between ARCHANGEL MICHAEL and SATAN. How could there have been A WAR in "A PERFECT PLACE" like HEAVEN? This sounds like the musings of MORTAL or HUMAN "SCRIPTURE WRITERS."

LAWSUITS are the legal means for POOR PEOPLE to get some of the MONEY of THE RICH.

Most GRAVES are not "SIX FEET UNDERGROUND."

If we knew about THE PRIVATE LIVES of SOME PUBLIC PEOPLE WE IDOLIZE, we would no longer IDOLIZE THEM.

No one WANTS TO DIE, that's why COURAGE or BRAVERY is defined as LOOKING DEATH IN THE EYE.

When some people say they don't have THE MONEY or THE TIME they are LYING. We can generally find THE MONEY or MAKE THE TIME to do anything we seriously want to do.

When POLICE OFFICERS misbehave, THE LEADERSHIP are always quick to say that their behavior does not reflect the entire force. But we don't always KNOW THAT.

We do not always LEARN FROM OUR MISTAKES, because we can't always admit THAT WE HAVE MADE A MISTAKE.

We are quick to REGRET that we don't have what others HAVE, but rarely are THANKFUL that we have some things that others DON'T HAVE.

POLLS and SURVEYS tend TO BELIEVE whatever PEOPLE TELL THEM.

The smallest NEGATIVE or POSITIVE gesture of a SUPERSTAR CELEBRITY is FRONT PAGE NEWS.

BULLDOGS are "THE CUTEST" UGLY DOGS.

Some PROSTITUTES have met some of "THE PILLARS OF THE COMMUNITY."

People may not be "ABOVE THE LAW," but some people are more HIGHLY VALUED than others: As NUNS are more Valued than PROSTITUTES.

We cannot claim to LOVE OURSELVES, if we want to be SOMEONE ELSE.

SPORTS or ATHLETICS for some males are "MANHOOD CONTESTS."

ALL ROMANTIC RELATIONSHIPS are MOSTLY HEALTHY or MOSTLY UNHEALTHY.

THE MAJOR BIOLOGICAL or PHYSICAL REASON FOR MALES AND FEMALES TO APPROACH ONE ANOTHER IS PRIMARILY TO ENGAGE IN SEX; any other reason they come together, must be "SPIRITUAL."

MALES and FEMALES can be "PLATONIC FRIENDS," if they both HAVE NO INTEREST IN HAVING SEX with ONE ANOTHER.

STRAIGHT FEMALES often get along well WITH HOMOSEXUAL MALES, because there is no "SEXUAL TENSION."

We are WHAT WE HAVE DONE IN LIFE, and WHAT LIFE HAS DONE TO US.

We tend to WANT TO EARN the MOST MONEY for DOING THE LEAST AMOUNT of WORK.

Almost everyone, RELIGIOUS or NONRELIGIOUS, describes or defines "BLESSINGS" and "SUCCESS" in terms of MONEY or NICE MATERIAL THINGS.

We are sometimes willing to "LIVE" with our SILENCE, rather than speak what "WE ARE DYING TO SAY."

Some WOMEN don't want TO PLAY some GAMES, because "SOMEONE COULD GET HURT"; and some MEN are willing to PLAY GAMES, despite the possibility of BEING HURT.

In "THE LAND OF THE IGNORANT," it is THE KNOWLEDGEABLE PEOPLE who are DISADVANTAGED.

No one is going through NOTHING, because EVERYONE, at some point, is GOING THROUGH SOMETHING.

Some of us enjoy TRYING or DOING things that are DANGEROUS; it makes US feel BRAVE but those WHO DON'T SURVIVE, or SUCCEED are "FOOLS."

OUR LIVES are what WE HAVE BEEN THROUGH, and WHAT HAS BEEN THROUGH US.

We do not always mean COMPLIMENTS or INSULTS.

The EXPERTS keep TELLING US TO TALK TO OUR ADOLESCENTS, about SEX. What do they think THE PARENTS NEED TO LEARN?

## RIGHT CAN BE WRONG

We tend to ASSUME that people who have been married for a long time are "HAPPY," and people who have a lot of children are "GREAT PARENTS."

BEYOND a LIVING WAGE, it doesn't matter HOW MUCH MONEY we MAKE, it ONLY MATTERS what WE MAKE with OUR MONEY.

There are TWO KINDS of RICH PEOPLE: those who have A LOT OF MONEY, and THOSE WHO OWE NO ONE.

Is it BETTER to FEEL what WE THINK, or to THINK about WHAT WE FEEL?

Can ANY OF OUR RIGHTS, ever BE WRONG?

Some LEADERS are BEING LED by THEIR FOLLOWERS.

It is "SELFISH" to accuse people of "BEING SELFISH" because THEY WON'T DO SOMETHING FOR OURSELVES.

We cannot UNDERSTAND why anyone would LIKE or DO what we would not like or do. Sometimes, the problem is not THEM; the PROBLEM is US.

CELEBRITIES are mostly known by "FAKE NAMES" – and few people EVER KNOW "THE REAL PERSONS."

We are "ALL VERY SIMILAR" people, trying desperately TO PROVE THAT "WE ARE DIFFERENT."

OUR "GREATEST PROBLEM" IS OUR INABILITY "TO SEE OUR GREATEST PROBLEMS."

STEREOTYPING or PREJUDICE is taking something MINOR about a people or a person and making it MAJOR.

When "PUSH COMES TO SHOVE," things have "GOTTEN OUT OF HAND."

SIMPLIFYING our lives is COMPLICATED.

Can "BLESSINGS" and "SUCCESS" ever be defined, without meaning "ACQUIRING A LOT OF MONEY?"

Some PEOPLE will not THINK we ARE INTERESTING, unless WE TAKE some INTEREST in THEIR INTERESTS.

We want TO HELP people SO MUCH, that we sometimes FORGET TO ENCOURAGE THEM to HELP THEMSELVES.

In MOST WARS, do PEOPLES MOSTLY FIGHT ONE ANOTHER, or do "LEADERS" MOSTLY FIGHT ONE ANOTHER?

Is SUCCESS HAPPINESS or is HAPPINESS SUCCESS?

NO RACE or ETHNIC GROUP OWNS AMERICA, because AMERICA is NOT JUST A COUNTRY—IT IS AN IDEA and AN IDEAL.

Some of us perceive CELEBRITIES as being RICH and GLAMOROUS, and NOT HAVING TO WORK HARD.

When we say, "AMERICA IS THE GREATEST COUNTRY, EVER." This does not mean that AMERICA IS NOT CAPABLE OF WRONG-DOING.

If we KNEW EVERYTHING that EVERYONE said about us BEHIND OUR BACKS, NO ONE would be able to get along with ANYONE. In private, EVERYONE CRITICIZES EVERYONE, except THEMSELVES.

EVERYONE does not "DESERVE" to be "HAPPY" or "SUCCESSFUL"; they deserve the right TO TRY TO BE.

Not all "THE GOOD OLD DAYS" were ALL THAT GOOD.

One does not always BECOME WISER WITH AGE; some BECOME SADDER, DUMBER and MORE CONFUSED.

The MORE we "NEED" to be FAMOUS, the LESS we NEED to be FAMOUS.

In WAR TIMES EVERYONE cries out FOR PEACE; in PEACE TIMES, we do things that CAUSE WAR.

When RICH or FAMOUS PEOPLE make large donations to POOR PEOPLE, is it PHILANTHROPY or GOOD PUBLIC RELATIONS?

Those of US who are HOPEFUL, tend to be TOO HOPEFUL, and those WHO ARE FEARFUL tend to be TOO FEARFUL.

There is NO "PRICE" that FEMALES won't PAY to LOOK BETTER, and NO "PRICE" men won't PAY to OBTAIN MORE MONEY.

We are BLESSED and CURSED by MONEY.

Regardless of our PERSONAL PURPOSES for our lives, THE GENERAL PURPOSE of every person IS TO BE THE BEST PERSON THEY CAN BE.

Most of us CANNOT receive GREAT PRAISE or GREAT GLORY, without it "SWELLING OUR HEADS."

We tend to experience ALL CRITICISM and CONDEMNATION as being TOO HARSH, and ALL PRAISE and GLORIFICATION, as NOT ENOUGH.

*RIGHT CAN BE WRONG*

ALL PRESIDENTS and SOME POLITICIANS receive CREDIT and BLAME that they DO NOT DESERVE.

Is ORGANIZED RELIGION trying to HELP US, or CONTROL US?

We all want CREDIT for SAVING PEOPLE, HELPING PEOPLE or CHANGING LIVES.

When we are trying to FORGET OUR PAST, sometimes OUR PAST REMEMBERS US.

We often HEED what we don't NEED, and NEED what we don't HEED.

We want to return to our "THEN" TIMES, with our "NOW" KNOWLEDGE.

We don't want to SEE OUR entire FUTURE, only THE GOOD PARTS.

THINGS CAN NEVER BE exactly AS THEY ONCE WERE.

We want to assist and raise up THE LOWLY, but we still want to FEEL SUPERIOR TO THEM.

We like SEEING DRAMA, but NOT OUR OWN.

The BETTER WAY to EDUCATE our CHILDREN is to BETTER EDUCATE OURSELVES.

Will INTER-RACIAL MARRIAGES or MISCEGENATION be what SOFTENS AMERICA from its seemingly intractable RACIAL SCHISM?

We do not CHOOSE OUR RELIGION; our RELIGION CHOOSES US. We GET IT from OUR PARENTS.

We think that what WE BELIEVE must BE RIGHT or GOOD, because SO MANY OTHER PEOPLE BELIEVE IT TOO.

Should MARRIAGE be the objective of every ROMANTIC RELATIONSHIP? Some people STAY TOGETHER LONGER, if they "LIVE IN SIN."

Is it still "DEMOCRACY" if AMERICANS elects AN AUTHORITARIAN or A TYRANT TO THE PRESIDENCY?

Why is PAYING FOR SEX so much more EGREGIOUS than getting it WITHOUT PAYING MONEY?

Our lives are PHYSICALLY MOTIVATED by our desire FOR FOOD, MONEY and SEX.

IN AMERICA, "SEX SELLS," but SELLING SEX is AGAINST THE LAW.

CITIES can REGULATE what happens IN PUBLIC, but should they be regulating SEXUAL BEHAVIOR?

SEX is sometimes "A BARGAINING TOOL," MOST PEOPLE PAY FOR SEX in SOME FORM; SEX is RARELY "FREE."

Once upon a time, some people GOT MARRIED, in order TO HAVE SEX.

Very FEW WOMEN give SEX, WITHOUT WANTING SOMETHING in RETURN.

Most WOMEN will not let MEN JUST "HIT IT AND QUIT IT."

MARRIAGE ITSELF, is "A SEXUAL ARRANGEMENT."

MARRIAGE is MOSTLY based on LOVE, LOOT or LUST.

Some people SHOULD BE FORGIVEN for their INFIDELITY, and SOME PEOPLE SHOULD NOT.

There is no COMMON SENSE as to what constitutes "COMMON SENSE."

If something makes us FEEL "REAL GOOD," it will be declared to be "REAL BAD."

The word "IMAGE" mostly means, "A VISUAL REPRESENTATION," what does "IN GOD'S IMAGE" MEAN?

Must GOD always be referred to as "A HE?"

All TEEN-AGERS come from a different place IN TIME and speak A DIFFERENT LANGUAGE.

Why isn't EARLY RELIGIOUS INSTRUCTION a form of "BRAINWASHING?"

MOST ROMANTICS always ASSUME that they already possess THE QUALITIES they seek in another.

Is STRENGTH OF CHARACTER proven in COMFORT or LUXURY or is it proven IN STRESS and STRUGGLE?

We cannot always DO WHAT WE WANT; we can always DO WHAT WE CAN.

PRETEXTS are USUALLY OUT OF CONTEXTS.

No matter how much WE PRAY, "ALL THINGS will EITHER GET BETTER or WORSE."

ALL PEOPLE are ALL DIFFERENT and ALL THE SAME

*RIGHT CAN BE WRONG*

ALL PEOPLE are DIFFERENT on "THE OUTSIDE," and ALL THE SAME on "THE INSIDE."

Most things in LIFE, involves SEX, MONEY, FOOD, and A DESIRE for POWER or GLORY.

We do not necessarily "DISLIKE" everything that WE DO NOT LIKE.

It RARELY occurs to us that we are THE ONES WHO ARE WRONG.

We sometimes must ADMIT BEING WRONG, to BECOME RIGHT.

It is difficult for most MALES and FEMALES to THINK or LOOK at one another "NON SEXUALLY."

Once A WEEK most PREACHERS are "PREACHING TO THE CHOIR."

AT EVERY SABBATH SERVICE, when THE SPIRITUAL LEADERS are PREACHING about "THE EVIL DOERS" in THE WORLD; those present DO NOT THINK they are talking TO THEM. They BELIEVE they are talking to people WHO ARE NOT THERE.

Some people can LOOK US IN THE EYE and STILL LIE.

We can NEVER LOVE EVERYONE, but we can ALWAYS LOVE SOMEONE.

People who think that "AFFIRMATIVE ACTION" IGNORES QUALIFIED PEOPLE, forget that IT AIDES QUALIFIED PEOPLE WHO WOULD HAVE OTHERWISE BEEN IGNORED. In "A MELTING POT," WHITE PEOPLE CANNOT ALWAYS HAVE "THE ENTIRE PRIZE," even if qualified. The REAL SITUATION was that some people WERE DEPRIVED, for them to GAIN THEIR ADVANTAGES or QUALIFICATIONS.

If PEOPLE HAVE BENEFITED from A CORRUPT SYSTEM, they do not have to have PERSONAL KNOWLEDGE of it.

MESSAGE TO YOUNG PEOPLE: GREAT RELATIONSHIPS are not based on BEAUTIFUL BODIES; they are based on BEAUTIFUL SPIRITS.

It is difficult for us to POSSESS FAME, without FAME POSSESSING US.

FAME is so esteemed because "YOU'RE NOBODY 'TIL EVERYBODY LOVES YOU."

SOME HAPPY PEOPLE are NOT FAMOUS, and SOME FAMOUS PEOPLE are NOT HAPPY.

LOSS of their PRIVACY is the price CELEBRITIES PAY FOR FAME.

Trying to APPEAR LARGE tends to make us LOOK SMALL.

ANGER is the FLIP - SIDE of HURT.

LIFE is VERY SERIOUS, and VERY SILLY.

THE DEFINITION OF "CLASSY": To have that RARE ABILITY to be "NICE" to people who are "NASTY" to us.

THE DEFINITION OF "EDUCATED": When we take ourselves OUT OF SCHOOL and place school INSIDE OF US.

WHAT DO PEOPLE WHO WERE BORN BLIND DREAM ABOUT?

In AMERICA, BLACKS and WHITES DISTRUST ONE ANOTHER, for DIFFERENT REASONS.

Is anything WORST THAN DEATH and how would anyone know?

If we can RECEIVE GOOD THINGS from OUR PARENTS, WE CAN RECEIVE BAD THINGS.

People who always THINK THEY ARE RIGHT, can NEVER SEE THEIR WRONGS.

NATURE tricks us into having children by initially presenting them to us as CUTE and CUDDLY, and not informing us that they GROW UP to become TEEN-AGERS.

When it is OUR TURN to have children, no one tells us THAT ONE DAY they may TURN ON US.

POPULAR THINGS are not always GREAT, and GREAT THINGS are not always POPULAR.

We CHASTISE our children for BAD BEHAVIOR and fail to REWARD THEM for GOOD BEHAVIOR, because we think that good behavior IS NORMAL BEHAVIOR.

How we SEE OTHERS is HIGHLY INFLUENCED by HOW WE SEE OURSELVES.

HOW WELL "WE SEE" depends on HOW "BLIND" WE ARE.

We go through LIFE COMPARING OURSELVES to ONE ANOTHER.

Should AMERICAN POLITICAL ELECTIONS be MORE THAN "POPULARITY CONTESTS?"

ONLY "CHILDREN" want to only do "WHAT THEY FEEL LIKE DOING."

When we PUT PEOPLE DOWN, we are telling them THAT WE THINK WE ARE BETTER THAN THEM, or think, THEY THINK THEY ARE BETTER THAN US.

*RIGHT CAN BE WRONG*

Great BOOKS are not always BEST SELLERS, and BEST SELLERS are not ALWAYS GREAT BOOKS.

If we DON'T KNOW "WHO WE ARE," we are either RUNNING AWAY FROM OURSELVES or TRYING TO FIND OURSELVES.

In THE HUMAN ANIMAL, "SEX IS BASIC," it is so hard TO CONTROL SEX, because SEX has SO MUCH CONTROL OVER US.

MANY of us have A LOVE/HATE relationship with SEX.

SEX is "A DOUBLE-EDGED SWORD," that we cannot seem "TO GET A HANDLE ON."

There is ABSOLUTELY NOTHING on which "WE CAN ALL AGREE."

Sometimes "the losers" WIN.

PARENTS LEARN from their PARENTING MISTAKES, but OUR CHILDREN SUFFER FROM THEM.

We could GET INTO A LOT OF TROUBLE, IF WE COULD NOT LIE.

In AMERICA, if we aren't RICH, FAMOUS, POWERFUL or HIGHLY CREDENTIALED, most people WILL NOT LISTEN TO US.

Many, if not MOST PEOPLE, don't think we can be HAPPY or SUCCESSFUL, unless WE are RICH and FAMOUS.

Do you believe that we sometimes "HAVE TO HURT, BEFORE WE CAN HEAL?"

Some STATE LOTTERIES are A SCAM for THE PUBLIC, and "A CASH COW" for STATES.

Don't believe those people who say, "SOMEONE HAS TO WIN" lotteries; This is NOT TRUE, some days NOBODY WINS, but THE STATE.

The best thing ADULTS CAN BECOME is THE BEST of WHO THEY ALREADY ARE.

WHITE PEOPLE are more apt to BLAME BLACK PEOPLE for NOT MATCHING THEM, than they are to take responsibility for DEPRIVING BLACK PEOPLE of THE ABILITY TO MATCH THEM.

Is there ANYTHING better to WORK FOR than MONEY?

BEING YOUNG is such "A DANGEROUS PLACE," because WE THINK WE KNOW, but WE DO NOT KNOW, and do not KNOW WHAT WE DO NOT KNOW.

THE LESS we KNOW the more we tend to BELIEVE we KNOW.

If "HATE SPEECH" is NOT ALLOWED, does that mean that ALL SPEECH must be "LOVE SPEECH?"

Most of us ARE NOT YOUNG ENOUGH to believe WE KNOW EVERYTHING.

THE YOUNG believe they are SO SMART, because we have raised them with FANTASIES, FAIRY TALES, INFINITES and ABSOLUTES.

Some WHITE PEOPLE TODAY, do not believe that PEOPLES WHOSE HANDS and FEET were TIED, deserve ANY CONSIDERATION IN DECIDING WHO WINS "THE HUMAN RACE."

Treating EVERYONE FAIRLY or JUSTLY, does not ALWAYS MEAN treating EVERYONE EQUALLY or THE SAME.

We cannot HELP BELIEVING that GOD must THINK and FEEL JUST LIKE US.

Prior to marriage, MALES tend to GO ALONG with WHATEVER THE FEMALE WANTS; IT IS THE AFTERMATH THAT IS SO TURBULENT.

FEMALES tend to have the need TO EXPLAIN WHY THEY ARE LEAVING A RELATIONSHIP; MALES DO NOT.

When we HIGHLY DEPEND ON HIGH TECH DEVICES, they become "THE MASTERS," and we become "THE SLAVES."

People WE LIKE can rarely say anything DUMB, and people WE DISLIKE, can never say anything SMART.

We are RARELY SATISFIED, we are constantly trying to become BIGGER, BETTER, BRIGHTER and RICHER.

A "FALLIBLE" JUSTICE SYSTEM IS ALWAYS TO BE FEARED, because ON OCCASION the INNOCENTS are CONVICTED and THE GUILTY GO FREE.

Not ALL OF THE POOR are deserving of our SYMPATHY or COMPASSION; SOME are SAINTS and SOME are CRIMINALS or SINNERS.

Almost EVERYONE has A DIFFERENT PLAN TO "SAVE THE WORLD," and when all these plans CONVERGE or CONFLATE, they tend to cause VIOLENCE or WARS, which "DIMINISHES THE WORLD."

*RIGHT CAN BE WRONG*

We cannot EXPECT MOST PEOPLE to HELP or ASSIST US; MOST PEOPLE are ONLY INTERESTED IN HELPING or ASSISTING THEMSELVES.

The person WHO PREACHES THE MOST, is sometimes the one WHO PRACTICES THE LEAST.

FEAR, ANGER or GUILT usually MAKES THE WRONG DECISION.

"TALK IS CHEAP," except ON TELEVISION, RADIO and other MEDIA.

Once we become STARS, someone will want to see us FALL.

The HIGHER we RISE, the Harder will be ANY FALL.

What we FAIL to receive in CHILDHOOD from PARENTS, we seek IN ADULTHOOD from THE WORLD.

We tell "LIES" to get to meet one another during COURTSHIP, then DEMAND "TRUTH" in the RELATIONSHIP.

The next person who tells you that MARRIAGE is only some meaningless WRITING ON PAPER, ask them to give you that meaningless paper IN THEIR WALLET.

Do they deserve more COMPASSION and LESS DISDAIN: Those scantily clad females we see on BIG CITY street corners, trying to SELL THE ONLY THING in their lives that they believe is of ANY VALUE?

We desperately need to PRACTICE MORE and PREACH LESS; anyone can say "I LOVE YOU" or "I BELIEVE IN GOD."

We tend to want TO TALK ABOUT WHAT WE BELIEVE, rather than TRY TO LIVE or DEMONSTRATE WHAT WE BELIEVE.

Sometimes we do not choose TO WANT WHAT WE NEED, but we certainly act as though WE NEED WHAT WE WANT.

In America, GREAT FAME and WEALTH are not necessarily indicative of ANYTHING.

Some people BELIEVE that ALL WESTERN RELIGIONS were derived from ROMAN and GREEK MYTHOLOGY.

GREAT WEALTH and GREAT LOVE are often INCOMPATIBLE, because we can DO THINGS for MONEY that LOVE WILL NOT ALLOW.

LIFE does not ALWAYS PRACTICE what "WE PREACH."

Are "THE HOLY BOOKS" the "WORDS OF GOD" or THE WORDS of ANCIENT GODLY MEN?

DOING THE RIGHT THING, is NO GUARANTEE that THINGS WON'T GO WRONG.

THE DEVIL HAS "DISCIPLES" TOO.

If THE DEVIL HIMSELF ran in AN AMERICAN ELECTION, he would receive SOME SUPPORT.

Trying TOO HARD to be HAPPY can make us VERY SAD.

Everyone solves THE SAME problems, DIFFERENTLY.

Some people are "ELOQUENTLY IGNORANT."

WELL FED, WELL BRED, and WELL READ, is a life WELL LED.

Are we GENUINELY RELATED to some of our RELATIVES, if we NEVER SEE THEM?

We do not RELATE WELL to some of our RELATIVES, because THEY are NOT "THE CHOSEN ONES."

RACE, RELATIVES and RELIGION are FORCED ON US.

Some HIGHLY EDUCATED people have NO CREDENTIALS, and some people with CREDENTIALS are not HIGHLY EDUCATED.

The two things that most UPSET US are VICIOUS LIES and THE UNFLATTERING TRUTHS.

EVIL PEOPLE call THE TRUTH, FALSE and promote what is FALSE, as THE TRUTH.

We cannot get along well with A MATE, unless we can occasionally GET ALONG WELL without them.

Do "TRADITIONS" represent OUR DESIRE to remain THE SAME.

THE HARM done to BLACK PEOPLE during SLAVERY is "UNFATHOMABLE."

We cannot always ASSUME that ALL RELIGIOUS LEADERS have GOOD or GODLY INTENTIONS.

If we knew THE BEST WAY to raise our children, would there be so many books telling us THE BEST WAY TO RAISE OUR CHILDREN?

We "HELP" some PEOPLE by NOT HELPING THEM.

Almost no one is willing to admit to A RICH or HAPPY CHILDHOOD; it is more IMPRESSIVE to tell people, "WE WERE POOR and STRUGGLED."

RIGHT CAN BE WRONG

"WHY DON'T YOU WRITE A BOOK?"

If we are RAISED within A POOR MILIEU, it does bother us, because EVERYONE IS POOR.

SMALL CHILDREN are NOT IMPRESSED by MONEY and GLITTERING MATERIALS.

Some people TAKE PRAISES or COMPLIMENTS, but DO NOT GIVE THEM.

We must DIVEST ourselves of the notion that only GOOD PEOPLE are ADMIRED; note the numbers of BANDITS and GANGSTERS who are ADMIRED.

Some of us THINK BEFORE WE SPEAK, some of us THINK WHILE WE ARE SPEAKING, and some of us ONLY THINK, AFTER WE HAVE SPOKEN.

A LOT of people talk about A LOT OF THINGS that they do not know A LOT ABOUT.

FEAR of being WRONG, stops some of us from DOING WHAT IS RIGHT.

Anyone who IDOLIZES or DEIFIES a HUMAN will be BETRAYED by their HUMANNESS.

Some of us lose WHAT WE HAVE trying to get WHAT WE WANT.

We tend to WANT TO BE LIKE SOMEONE ELSE or WANT SOMEONE ELSE TO BE LIKE US.

A LOVING RELATIONSHIP with SOMEONE ELSE gives us INSIGHTS INTO OURSELVES.

AMERICA is reluctant to reveal the TRUE HISTORY of BLACK PEOPLE, because it is SO DARK.

MANY RELIGIOUS PEOPLE are "NOT SAINTS," they just THINK THEY ARE.

We tend to believe THAT WE ARE BETTER THAN OTHERS, just because WE ARE BETTER OFF than others.

RACISM and PREJUDICE are "IGNORANT," because THEY BLAME PEOPLE for the way THEY WERE BORN.

The only way to ABSOLUTELY KNOW what anyone really thinks of us, is to NOT BE IN THE ROOM when they talk about us.

If we do not LISTEN to what WE HEAR, we have NOT HEARD IT.

WHAT has more POWER and INFLUENCE in THE WORLD: MONEY or RELIGION?

THE BEST GOAL is PERFECTION, because IT CAN NEVER BE REACHED.

Most GREAT PARENTS are "OVERLY PROTECTIVE," and NO ONE BLAMES THEM FOR IT BUT THEIR CHILDREN.

HOLY BOOKS are sometimes CONTRADICTORY, because they were written by various people who did not "COMPARE NOTES."

RELIGIOUS PEOPLE pray for MONEY, and NICE THINGS, as much as they pray for ETERNAL LIFE or HEAVEN.

LIFE is always UNPREDICTABLE, offers us NO GUARANTEES, is UNFAIR and DOES NOT ALWAYS MAKE SENSE, but THERE IS NO ALTERNATIVE.

To have been EDUCATED in THE ANCIENT WORLD, one had to be well versed in ROMAN, GREEK and some other ANCIENT CIVILIZATIONS. And many of the SCRIBES and RELIGIOUS LEADERS who wrote THE SCRIPTURES were EDUCATED in these traditions. And since THESE GREAT CIVILIZATIONS preceded THE CHRISTIAN ERA, one can see their influence in some of THE HOLY BOOKS. HADES (the underworld abode of the dead) in CREEK MYTHOLOGY, in ORGANIZED RELIGION became HELL. Another large event in some ANCIENT TRADITIONS, was the idea of "A HUMAN SACRIFICE"; in ORGANIZED RELIGION, this became JESUS CHRIST.

THE WORLD'S THREE GREAT WESTERN RELIGIONS, ALL EMANATED FROM THE SAME SOURCE.

Some RELIGIOUS LEADERS are not JUST TEACHING and PREACHING THEIR BELIEFS, they are TEACHING and PREACHING THEIR IGNORANCE.

THE OBVIOUS, OBVIOUSLY is NOT ALWAYS OBVIOUS.

Sometimes, IN A FREE SOCIETY, we have A RIGHT to BE WRONG.

COLLOQUIALLY, FEMALES always have MORE TO SAY, than MALES.

Is there ANY DOUBT that SOME POLITICIANS care MORE ABOUT THEMSELVES than they CARE ABOUT US?

If we marry A PREVIOUSLY MARRIED PERSON, their EX-SPOUSE probably knows more about them than we do.

No one is SMART or WISE enough TO DO WHATEVER THEY WANT TO DO, WELL.

*RIGHT CAN BE WRONG*

How do you think THE RICH PREACHERS in AMERICA would do IN THE THIRD WORLD?

Do you think RICH PREACHERS rate or measure THEMSELVES by HOW MANY SOULS they "SAVE," or HOW MANY SEATS THEY FILL?

Are RICH PREACHERS RICH, because THEY HAVE "CAPTURED an AUDIENCE," in THE RICHEST COUNTRY in THE WORLD?

When we feel SAFE AGAIN, we never KEEP OUR PROMISES TO GOD.

The MORAL and POWER DICHOTOMY in THE UNIVERSE is expressed in many ways: The struggle between GOOD and EVIL. The fight between GOD and SATAN, RIGHT and WRONG, LIGHT and DARKNESS, TRUTH and LIES, and NEGATIVE and POSITIVE.

When most people express their GENERAL opinions on MARRIAGE, DIVORCE, POLITICS, SEX, RACE and RELIGION, they are mostly talking about themselves SPECIFICALLY.

Most of OUR LEADERS, TEACHERS and PREACHERS, want to be RICH AND FAMOUS TOO.

We tend to believe that whatever life we are living is "OUR BEST LIFE," until we start LIVING A BETTER LIFE.

NO ONE can tell PEOPLE how to "LIVE THEIR BEST LIVES," unless THEY KNOW WHAT IS BEST FOR EVERYONE.

SEX IS "NATURAL," but MARRIAGE IS NOT, but is our attempt to TRANSCEND our ANIMAL INSTINCTS, and become MORE HUMAN or MORE LOVING.

It is not ALWAYS best to TELL THE TRUTH; it is always best to know WHEN it is BEST TO TELL THE TRUTH.

EVIL PEOPLE can do things to us that LOVING PEOPLE are not MORALLY ALLOWED TO DO TO THEM.

We only KNOW OURSELVES and OTHERS in DEGREES, and NO ONE COMPLETELY KNOWS ANYONE.

Some RICH and FAMOUS people do not like their work, THEY JUST LIKE THEIR MONEY.

OUR HANDS are THE GREATEST "TOOL" ever CREATED.

LIFE and THE WORLD will NEVER BE precisely as WE WISH THEY WERE.

Parents SAY they want their children to receive THE BEST EDUCATION. But parents do not want their children to receive ANY EDUCATION that causes them TO DOUBT or QUESTION THEIR PARENT'S BELIEFS and VALUES

Are they "THE WORDS of GOD," or do they CLAIM they are "THE WORDS OF GOD," to get us to BELIEVE THEM MORE?

BELIEVING is not KNOWING and FAITH is not necessarily FACT.

Not all our THINKING is done with OUR HEADS, some is done WITH OUR HEARTS or EMOTIONS.

FANS do not LOVE THEIR "IDOLS"; they LOVE WHAT THEY HAVE ATTAINED

It is sometimes DIFFICULT to APPRECIATE what WE HAVE, because we are DISTRACTED BY WHAT WE WANT.

There is an INTELLECTUAL DEFINITION of GOD and LOVE, and there is an EMOTIONAL DEFINITION.

Every time WE SPEAK, we tell others WHO WE ARE, regardless of WHAT WE SAY.

When others physically ATTACK US, we want "JUSTICE"; but when we ATTACK OTHERS, we want "MERCY."

All LOVERS HAVE SEX, but ALL SEX IS NOT LOVING.

If THE SEX is NOT LOVING, is it HONEST to call it "MAKING LOVE?"

Some of us RESENT MAJOR HOLIDAYS, because WE DON'T WANT TO BE TOLD HOW TO ACT or WHAT TO DO.

EVERYONE is IGNORANT regarding SOMETHING.

In AMERICA, almost "ANYONE" can become RICH, FAMOUS or PRESIDENT.

The MOST DANGEROUS "ANIMAL" in existence is THE HUMAN ONE.

It is SO DIFFICULT to REACH "THE TOP," because SO MANY ARE APPLYING FOR THAT POSITION.

In AMERICA, the RICH preachers PREACH SUCCESS and HAPPINESS; in THE THIRD WORLD, the poor preachers PREACH EATING and SURVIVAL.

THE LARGER WORLD is composed of MANY smaller WORLDS.

The DESIRE FOR GLORY causes some of us to do some INGLORIOUS THINGS.

# RIGHT CAN BE WRONG

"O' LORD, FORGIVE US OUR SELFISHNESS, PETTINESS, INTOLERANCE, AND LACK OF LOVE, AND PLEASE KEEP OUR NEIGHBORHOOD WHITE."

RELIGIOUS PEOPLE seek the GLORY and APPROVAL of THEIR GOD; POLITICIANS seek THE SAME FROM THEIR VOTERS.

We cannot DO ANYTHING GREAT, unless we are WILLING TO UPSET SOME PEOPLE.

Everyone NEEDS SOMEONE to TALK TO, without having TO "MONITOR" their EVERY WORD.

THE BETTER MARRIAGES are between "TWO GIVERS," and THE WORST MARRIAGES are between "TWO TAKERS."

CHANGE is SO DIFFICULT because SO MANY PEOPLE have A VESTED INTEREST in THINGS REMAINING THE SAME.

We cannot "BE" ROMANTICALLY WITH SOMEONE, UNLESS we know when to LEAVE THEM ALONE.

We think WE KNOW CELEBRITIES, just because WE KNOW A LOT ABOUT CELEBRITIES.

WE LAUGH at people who have SLIGHT PHYSICAL DEFORMITIES, and FEEL SORRY for those with MAJOR ONES

We think PHYSICAL ILLNESS is SAD, but MENTAL ILLNESS, is FUNNY.

Do you think "I LOVE YOU," is spoken TOO EASILY and TOO OFTEN; so that it has become ALMOST MEANINGLESS?

CELEBRITIES do not have full OWNERSHIP of THEIR LIVES; SOME OF THEIR LIVES BELONG TO US.

The best time to reproduce children is WHEN WE ARE YOUNG; but the best time to raise children is WHEN WE ARE OLDER or MORE MATURE.

## RIGHT CAN BE WRONG

We only BULLY PEOPLE we PERCEIVE TO BE WEAKER than US. If A LARGER MAN had been on "THAT STAGE," a certain ACTOR, would not have GONE ON STAGE TO SLAP HIM.

Do ELDERLY PEOPLE have A RIGHT to complain about POPULAR MUSIC, is THEY DON'T BUY POPULAR MUSIC?

Do you think MOST RICH CELEBRITIES seem "ARROGANT" or NOT? Do you think THEY THINK they are BETTER than THE REST OF US?

MONEY ALONE cannot do many GREAT THINGS; the greatest things we do with money, IS SPEND IT, GIVE IT AWAY or FLAUNT IT.

BLACK and WHITE are NOT COLORS.

LIFE IS SO COMPLEX, that WE LIKE or LOVE some "SINNERS," and DISLIKE some of the SELF-RIGHTEOUS or SANCTIMONIOUS "SAINTS."

People who are genuinely GREAT, SAINTLY, HEROES or GENIUSES, never DESCRIBE THEMSELVES AS SUCH.

Most of us are trying to "OUT-DO" one another, "RE-DO" one another or "DO" one another.

We do not ALWAYS CHOOSE what we do IN LIFE, sometimes LIFE CHOOSES.

What we "LEAST EXPECT" is more likely TO HAPPEN to us than WHAT WE MOST FEAR.

DEATH and TAXES are not THE SUREST THINGS in life, because some people do not pay taxes; THE SUREST THINGS IN LIFE, are "DEATH," "RAIN" and "CHANGE."

Only STRONG PEOPLE can admit to their WEAKNESSES.

Sometimes WE CRY, but DON'T KNOW WHY.

Some people are MORE ADAMANT in DEFENDING their PREJUDICES, than THEIR PRINCIPLES.

BEING BUSY is not necessarily BEING PRODUCTIVE.

Which IS BETTER or WORSE: TO BELIEVE LIES or TO NOT BELIEVE THE TRUTH?

"ADULT CHILDREN" sounds like AN OXYMORON.

The question is not, CAN ROMANTICS LOVE ONE ANOTHER, but CAN THEY "SUSTAIN" THEIR LOVE OVER TIME?

We should not be TREATING ALL CHILDREN THE SAME, because ALL CHILDREN ARE DIFFERENT.

The worst thing we can do to AN EGO-CENTRIC MANIAC is TO IGNORE THEM.

Is ANY RELIGION BETTER than ANY OTHER RELIGION, and IF SO, WHAT MAKES THEM BETTER?

HUMAN BEHAVIOR is mostly AN ART, and not A SCIENCE, because NO ONE CAN EVER KNOW or PREDICT WHAT A HUMAN WILL or WON'T DO.

When we do not know how to solve a problem WE ENDLESSLY TALK or ANALYZE IT, until we develop "ANALYSIS PARALYSIS."

Is IT RATIONAL, FOR THE PUBLIC to keep expecting THE POLICE AUTHORITIES to be able to ARREST SOMEONE before THEY BECOME A SERIAL KILLER or MASS MURDERER? On

*RIGHT CAN BE WRONG*

WHAT BASIS can they be ARRESTED – FOR WHAT THEY MAY DO? Do we arrest them for being "A RED FLAG?"

It just SO ENRAGES US, that WE CANNOT MAKE our IMPERFECT LIVES, "PERFECT."

All LIFE is A FALLIBLE ADVENTURE, that is sometimes DANGEROUS, INSECURE and UNPREDICTABLE, and WE CANNOT ACCEPT THAT.

We cannot ACCEPT LIFE THE WAY IT IS, because we cannot stop WANTING IT TO BE THE WAY, WE WANT IT TO BE.

YOUNG PEOPLE have so much difficulty WITH RELATIONSHIPS, because THEY HAVE "NO PAST" TO INFORM THEM.

If some MONEY IS PAPER, and PAPER IS MADE FROM TREES, then maybe "MONEY DOES GROW ON TREES."

Some WOMEN only want a man FOR HIS MONEY, and some MEN only want a woman FOR HER HONEY.

Men who can only ATTRACT WOMEN with NICE CARS are ALWAYS RIDING ALONE.

When we are IN PUBLIC, there is always SOMEONE WATCHING US, that WE CAN'T SEE.

We can learn a lot about people BY WHAT THEY LAUGH ABOUT and WHAT THEY CRY ABOUT.

It is DANGEROUS to drive TOO FAST THROUGH LIFE and to drive TOO SLOWLY.

We are "LIVING A LIE" to the same degree that "WE CANNOT HANDLE THE TRUTH."

If we are OBSESSED with something SOCIALLY ACCEPTABLE, we will be said to be DEDICATED or COMMITTED; however, if we are OBSESSED with something NOT SOCIALLY ACCEPTABLE, we will be said to be HOPELESSLY "ADDICTED."

When EVERYONE believes THEY ARE RIGHT, things will usually TURN OUT WRONG.

How many COMMERCIAL MOVIES, BOOKS, PLAYS or MUSIC do you think can LIVE UP TO THEIR HYPE?

Nearly every NEW BOOK, SONG, MOVIE, PLAY or ANYTHING is hyped as "THE GREATEST EVER."

PUBLIC LIVES and PRIVATE LIVES almost NEVER MATCH.

When we say, "LIFE IS UNFAIR," we do not EXPECT for it TO BE UNFAIR TO US.

In THE SALES MARKETS TODAY, "QUALITY AND SUBSTANCE SUFFERS" because "POPULARITY SELLS."

If WE "GO DOWN," it will PROBABLY BE BECAUSE of OUR OBSESSION with SEX, MONEY and POWER.

WHY do WOMEN, tend to be MORE RELIGIOUS than MEN?

Some things that SOUND GOOD, are NOT "GOOD and SOUND."

THE LONGER A BRONZE STATUE stands in front of a government building, the more "INVISIBLE" it will become.

Some people do not mind GETTING OLDER, they just want TO LOOK YOUNGER.

THE MIND mostly remembers WHAT IS SAID, THE HEART only remembers HOW THINGS FELT.

We never REALLY KNOW what OUR LOVED ONES genuinely THINKS OF US; THEIR HEARTS won't ALLOW THEM TO TELL US.

Is EVERY FIGHT or DISPUTE between BLACK PEOPLE and WHITE PEOPLE, necessarily "A RACIAL INCIDENT?"

We tend to DISLIKE PEOPLE who LIE TOO MUCH, and people WHO ARE TOO HONEST.

We all have A NEED TO "CONNECT"; if we cannot do it SPIRITUALLY, we will DO IT SEXUALLY.

ULTIMATELY, what most of us most want from LIFE, is TO BE LIKED, LOVED, RESPECTED, ADMIRED and GLORIFIED.

It is THE IGNORED SMALL PROBLEMS that cause THE LARGE PROBLEMS.

Sometimes, WHEN WE MOSTLY THINK WE ARE RIGHT, we are MOSTLY WRONG.

Not only do we NOT FOLLOW THE GOLDEN RULE, but most of us believe OTHERS SHOULD DO MORE UNTO US THAN WE DO UNTO THEM.

It is difficult to interest THE YOUNG in "SOMETHING OLD," or THE ELDERLY in "SOMETHING NEW."

We are only AS LARGE, as the things THAT MAKE US FEEL SMALL.

*RIGHT CAN BE WRONG*

There is POSITIVE HONESTY or TRUTH and NEGATIVE HONESTY or TRUTH.

Our MINDS and our HEARTS are meant to SYMBIOTICALLY FUNCTION.

FEAR is "THE CHILD" of IGNORANCE.

Many POORLY EDUCATED PEOPLE are CONFUSED.

SMALL CHILDREN are LIVING PROOF, that THE LESS WE KNOW, THE MORE WE HAVE TO SAY.

We are not RIGHTEOUS or RELIGIOUS by what "WE PREACH"; we are by WHAT "WE PRACTICE."

It is DIFFICULT to believe SOME NEW THINGS, because to do so, WE MAY HAVE TO STOP BELIEVING SOME OLD THINGS.

We know WE DO NOT ALWAYS KNOW WHAT IS BEST FOR OURSELVES, Yet WE THINK WE KNOW WHAT IS BEST FOR OTHERS.

We PARENT our CHILDREN to THE LEVEL of OUR OWN MATURITY, SOPHISTICATION or EDUCATION.

For MOST OF US, "GOD" and "LOVE" are WHATEVER WE WANT GOD and LOVE TO BE.

We TAKE CARE of our children, until THEY REACH the age OF MAJORITY and WORRY ABOUT THEM ALL OF OUR LIVES.

Today, it is NOT ENOUGH to just BE "THE BEST," we must be "THE BEST SELLER."

We are always SEEKING SOMETHING, we just DON'T ALWAYS KNOW WHAT IT IS.

We are "ALL THE SAME" and "ALL DIFFERENT" and WE ALL think OUR DIFFERENCES make A DIFFERENCE.

Do YOU THINK THAT MONEY IS THE MOST IMPORTANT "thing" IN LIFE?

MESSAGE TO YOUNG PEOPLE: THE OUTSIDE ATTRACTS, but THE INSIDE is "WHO WE ARE."

Do most POLITICIANS want to "GIVE MORE POWER TO THE PEOPLE," or do they want MORE POWER OVER the PEOPLE?

To become "MORE INTERESTING," we must BECOME MORE INTERESTED.

PAST SLAVE TRADERS, RATIONALIZED or JUSTIFIED IT by TELLING THEMSELVES that THEY WERE "BRINGING SAVAGES to CHRISTIANITY."

THOMAS JEFFERSON once suggested that not only was SLAVERY WRONG, but that BLACK SLAVES may be capable of becoming equal to WHITES. NO ONE KNOWS HOW HE WAS ABLE TO GET AWAY WITH UTTERING SUCH 18TH CENTURY "NONSENSE."

IN WAR, the first thing we do IS "VILIFY" or "DEMONIZE" OUR ENEMIES. The WORST we MAKE THEM LOOK, the BETTER we LOOK.

No matter HOW ATROCIOUS our WAR ENEMIES WERE, after THE WAR, we tend TO "BEFRIEND THEM."

When you hear someone say, "Doctors don't know everything," tell them to go see THE PERSON WHO DOES.

It is not ALWAYS WISE to LISTEN TO OURSELVES; we cannot BELIEVE everything WE THINK.

SOME living children NEVER GROW UP.

All PROBLEMS are mostly PHYSICAL, ECONOMIC, or SPIRITUAL; and EACH ONE IMPACTS THE OTHER TWO.

WHERE IS GOD, during WORLD PLAGUES, ENSLAVEMENTS, HOLOCAUSTS, FAMINES, WARS, DEPRESSIONS, and NATURAL DISASTERS?

It is DIFFICULT to find A JOB or A PROFESSION that we LIKE or LOVE, and that ALSO PAYS US A LOT OF MONEY – WE GENERALLY TRADE ONE FOR THE OTHER.

LIFE can present us with PROBLEMS, which are not only "UNPRECEDENTED," but that we could NOT IMAGINE.

Do we want "A BETTER WORLD," or DO WE WANT LIFE and THE WORLD to be "WHAT WE WANT THEM TO BE?"

We think what WE WANT FOR THE WORLD, is "THE BETTER WORLD." The PROBLEM IS, everyone wants it to be SOMETHING DIFFERENT.

When we are POOR, the problem is, HOW DO WE BECOME RICH; when we are RICH, the problem is, HOW DO WE BEST HELP THE POOR.

RELIGION has made SOME PEOPLE "SANE" and SOME PEOPLE "INSANE."

*RIGHT CAN BE WRONG*

"I SWEAR, SOMETIMES I DON'T KNOW IF IT'S LOVE OR INSANITY."

Most POLITICIANS do not tell us what THEY THINK, BELIEVE or FEEL; they tell us what is most to THEIR ADVANTAGE to THINK, BELIEVE or FEEL.

We are ALL HUMAN-ANIMALS; our ANIMAL INSTINCTS are "MOSTLY SEXUAL"; however, OUR HUMAN MOTIVATIONS are TO BE "MORE LOVING."

The PROBLEMS we possess, WE PROJECT UNTO OTHERS.

CONTEMPORARY CITIZENS can rarely SEE ALL "THE WRONGS" OF THEIR OWN TIMES. Just as DURING SLAVERY, most people saw ABSOLUTELY NOTHING WRONG about it.

It is DIFFICULT to QUESTION THE STATUS QUO. We think things are the way THEY ARE, BECAUSE THEY ARE best the way they are.

In POP CULTURE, what's BEST is what is POPULAR, THIN, RICH, LOOKS GOOD, GLEAMS, SINGS, BEAMS and BLINGS.

Part of US wants to LIVE REALITY and part of US wants to LIVE in A WORLD of FANTASY.

Some YOUNG PEOPLE don't know THAT THEY WON'T ALWAYS LOOK THAT WAY.

Most CELEBRITIES are AFRAID of THE DARK, FAT, OLD and GRAY, perhaps this is why GRETA GARBO "wanted to be alone."

How do we DEFINE GREATNESS, and WHO DECIDES WHO POSSESSES IT?

How many people do you know who are TOTALLY SATISFIED with the way THEY LOOK?

When RELIGIOUS LEADERS experience things THEY DON'T UNDERSTAND they generally DECLARE THEM TO BE "A SIN."

GROWTH, EDUCATION, KNOWLEDGE, MATURITY, LOVE, FACTS, TRUTHS, WISDOM, JUSTICE, UNSELFISHNESS and SCIENCE are THE SOLUTIONS to MOST OF OUR PROBLEMS.

When we DON'T KNOW, we don't want ANYONE TO KNOW that WE DON'T KNOW.

Where MONEY is "KING," LOVE will be "A PEASANT."

Are MOST ADULT MALES interested in anything else OTHER THAN FOOD, MONEY, SEX and SPORTS?

Whenever A CAMERA is pointed at us, OUR FIRST DESIRE is TO LOOK GOOD, POSE or PERFORM.

Can you think of anything important IN AMERICA that is not "MEASURED IN MONEY?"

EVERYTHING is not "ALL IN OUR HEADS," but MOST THINGS ARE.

We only CARE ABOUT domesticated ANIMALS; animals IN THE WILD are ON THEIR OWN.

Another way WHITES JUSTIFIED SLAVERY, was to declare BLACK PEOPLE to be NOT HUMAN, because we can treat our "ANIMALS" any way we wish.

HOW CAN "ANTISEMITIC CHRISTIANS" HATE JEWS, WHEN THEIR RELIGION IS IN THE NAME OF A JEW?

We are ALL FUNCTIONING with VARYING DEGREES of "SANITY."

The more WE PREPARE for "A RAINY DAY," the less it is likely TO RAIN.

We can SEE AGING and WEIGHT GAIN in OTHERS, better than WE CAN SEE IT IN OURSELVES.

TELEVISION and OTHER MEDIA are in the UNENVIABLE POSITION of TRYING TO "PLEASE EVERYONE."

Is HAVING CHILDREN more A RIGHT or MORE A RESPONSIBILITY?

We are more likely "TO LIKE AT FIRST SIGHT," than "LOVE AT FIRST SIGHT."

Some MALES are NOT INTERESTED in FEMALES --- they are only INTERESTED in SEX.

Why do we feel that we have to HIT or ATTACK someone, just because they don't THINK, FEEL or BELIEVE the same as us? This desire mostly stems from OUR ANIMAL INSTINCTS.

It sometimes doesn't matter WHAT IS SAID or DONE, it only matters WHO SAID or DID IT.

The 'HEARTS" of some ATHEISTS want "TO BELIEVE," but THEIR "HEADS" WON'T LET THEM.

WHAT WE "BELIEVE," does not ALWAYS MAKE SENSE; what "MAKES SENSE," we don't ALWAYS WANT TO BELIEVE.

The BETTER WAY to understand PEOPLE WHO ARE LOST, is to REMEMBER WHEN WE WERE LOST.

"WAR" is HUMANKIND at ITS WORST, and LOVE and UNIVERSAL CONCERN are ALL OF US AT OUR BEST.

*RIGHT CAN BE WRONG*

Most RELIGIONISTS only PRAISE GOD ORALLY or VERBALLY. Is not THE BEST WAY TO PRAISE GOD, is FOR ALL OF US to SHOW MORE LOVING KINDNESS to ONE ANOTHER?

Sometimes, we don't know WHAT WE ARE CAPABLE OF, until something or someone PUSHES US.

The TWO GROUPS who are hardest for us to UNDERSTAND, are those WHO ARE NOT WELL EDUCATED, and those WHO ARE WELL EDUCATED.

Some of us TRY ON MANY SPOUSES, before WE FIND ONE THAT FITS.

We are NOT WITH OUR BEST MATE, unless being with THAT MATE makes US a BETTER PERSON.

We are not "A GOOD PERSON" unless we can BE KIND to "A BAD PERSON."

Some of us ask people to DO THINGS FOR US that WE WOULD NEVER DO FOR THEM.

AN "AVERAGE PERSON" doesn't want to be "AN AVERAGE PERSON."

Sometimes, when we hear BAD NEWS, WE BLAME THE MESSENGER, and IGNORE THE MESSAGE.

MOVIE STARS mostly portray roles as REGULAR PEOPLE, and REGULAR PEOPLE mostly dream that they are MOVIE STARS.

Perhaps SOME BLACK PEOPLE see RACISM where it DOES NOT EXIST, and perhaps A LOT of WHITE PEOPLE DO NOT see RACISM where IT DOES EXIST.

We cannot always SEE what someone SEES in SOMEONE ELSE, because we CANNOT SEE "HOW" THEY SEE or WHAT THEY ARE SEEING.

Do some MEGA CHURCHES invest more money IN HELPING OTHERS or IN HELPING THEMSELVES?

Most of us WOULD RATHER BE RIGHT, than LEARN SOMETHING FROM BEING WRONG.

When we caused ALL THAT DAMAGE, we were "ONLY TRYING TO HELP."

We pass OUR STRENGTHS and OUR WEAKNESSES to our CHILDREN.

YOUNG ROMANTICS find it MOST DIFFICULT to "LOOK BEYOND LOOKS."

DO BELIEFS mostly CONTRADICT FACTS, or DO FACTS mostly CONTRADICT BELIEFS?

THE BEST PEOPLE do not always KNOW WHAT IS BEST FOR THE PEOPLE.

The BEST PEOPLE are not ALWAYS in THE BEST JOBS.

What most people enjoy hearing ABOUT THE RICH and FAMOUS is that THEY ARE NO BETTER THAN THE REST OF US.

Were it not for THE LIVES OF CELEBRITIES, some people WOULD HAVE NO LIVES AT ALL.

Not everyone IS "QUALIFIED" to DO WHAT THEY DO.

All RACISM is PREJUDICE, but NOT ALL PREJUDICE is RACISM.

We "IDOLIZE" and "WORSHIP" one another SO INTENSELY, that we sometimes forget THAT WE ARE ALL "ONLY HUMAN."

YOUNG ADULTS are never good AT INTROSPECTION.

WHAT is MORE IMPORTANT: What is MOST IMPORTANT or TRUE, or WHAT MOST PEOPLE BELIEVE IS MOST IMPORTANT or TRUE? Is WHAT IS MOST IMPORTANT or TRUE JUST A MATTER OF OPINION?

Do you think "RELIGION" is RESPONSIBLE for more WAR or PEACE?

There are NO MARRIAGES "MADE IN HEAVEN," because all marriages ARE MADE ON EARTH.

No one is SMART ENOUGH, WISE ENOUGH or EDUCATED ENOUGH to know WHAT IS BEST FOR ALL OF US. Many RELIGIOUS PEOPLE do not "KNOW" MUCH ABOUT THEIR HOLY BOOKS or THEIR RELIGIONS; they mostly have AN EMOTIONAL ATTACHMENT TO THEM.

When we cannot answer difficult religious questions, the common response is, "GOD WORKS IN MYSTERIOUS WAYS." THEN WHY do so many people CLAIM TO KNOW THE WAYS OF GOD?

We tend to teach our children THE EXCEPTIONS, as though THEY WERE THE RULE.

When someone does something EXCEPTIONAL, we say, "ANYONE CAN DO IT."

We can't ALL BE RICH and FAMOUS or there would be NO ONE LEFT to ENVY, IDOLIZE and WORSHIP those WHO ARE.

*RIGHT CAN BE WRONG*

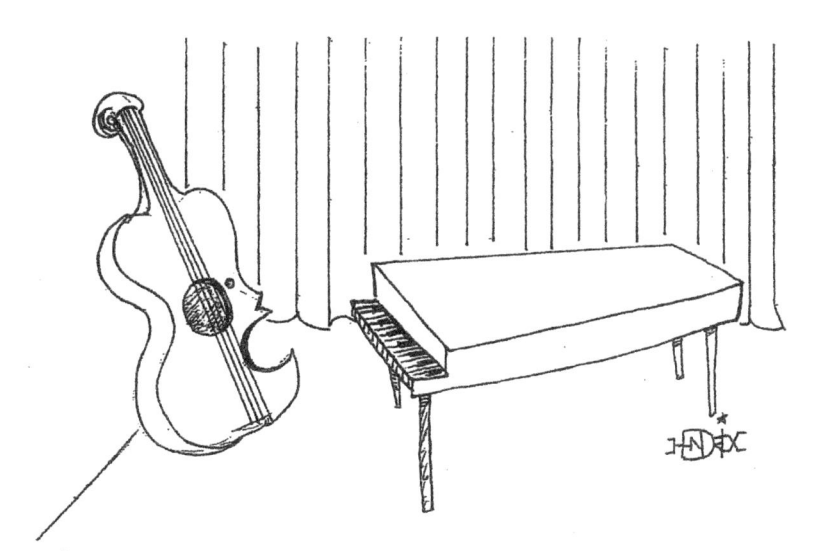

"AND I NOTICED LAST NIGHT......HE WAS PLAYING THE BLACK KEYS MORE THAN THE WHITE."

If there is ever "A JUDGMENT DAY," or A TIME OF ACCOUNTABILITY, we CAN NEVER BE SURE WE HAVE BEEN "GOOD ENOUGH."

Some people "NEVER GIVE UP," especially WHEN THEY SHOULD.

If we believe GOD HAS BLESSED US, by SAVING US from AN ACCIDENT, what do we say about those WHO DIED?

What "WE GET" doesn't make us AS HAPPY as what "WE GIVE."

The WORST TANGIBLE GIFT TO GIVE is to GIVE SOMEONE SOMETHING that WE WANT FOR OURSELVES.

Is BELIEF in HOLY BOOKS always an ALL or NOT AT ALL proposition?

We cannot SHOW PEOPLE their problems, if THEY CANNOT SEE THEM.

When we LAUGH or JOKE about things that people CANNOT CHANGE about themselves, we are saying WE THINK WE ARE SOMETHING BETTER.

NO ONE has it ALL FIGURED OUT, because ALL OF IT cannot BE FIGURED OUT.

We are NOT HELPING POOR PEOPLE, unless we are HELPING POOR PEOPLE NOT TO BE POOR.

Those ON THE LEFT, always THINK THEY ARE RIGHT, and those ON THE RIGHT, think that THEY ARE ALL THAT AMERICA HAS LEFT.

CELEBRITIES are always trying to "RAISE OUR AWARENESS" of things that WE ARE MORE THAN AWARE OF.

We ALL have our OWN VERSIONS of HAPPINESS, SUCCESS, BEAUTY, HEAVEN, HELL, LOVE, SATAN and GOD. And NOT ONE can BE "ABSOLUTELY" or DEFINITIVELY CORROBORATED, VALIDATED, SUBSTANTIATED or AUTHENTICATED, because we ALWAYS TRYING TO DO SO.

The DEFINITIONS of SOME "ABSTRACT TERMS" are "SO ELUSIVE," that we CANNOT "PEN THEM DOWN."

Whenever we DECLARE SOMETHING is SPECIAL or DEAR in LIFE, WE TRY TO ATTRIBUTE or PROJECT IT TO GOD.

Why can't we still HAVE COMPASSION, for people who cause their own problems or "WHO CAN ONLY BLAME THEMSELVES?"

PUBLIC LIFE sometimes ASKS US to "FORFEIT OUR PRIVATE LIFE" (this may be WHY so many CELEBRITIES are DIVORCED).

ORGANIZED RELIGION is TOO OLD and TOO SLOW, and SCIENCE and TECHNOLOGY are TOO NEW and TOO FAST.

Why do we NEVER FEEL SORRY for RICH PEOPLE? Do we THINK or BELIEVE that they never HAVE PROBLEMS, or they NEVER SUFFER because THEY HAVE MONEY?

We must FIND OUR PEACE and JOY WHEREVER and WHENEVER WE CAN. Because LIFE and THE WORLD are ALWAYS in CONFLICT or UPHEAVAL and are always FALLIBLE; there are always DIFFICULT QUESTIONS to ANSWER, TOUGH PROBLEMS to SOLVE, and COMPLEX SITUATIONS that MUST BE DEALT WITH.

If WE BELIEVE "EVERYTHING IS IN GOD'S HANDS," why do WE PRAY SO FERVENTLY FOR THINGS TO BE IN "OUR HANDS?"

We want YOUNG PEOPLE to "ACT OLDER," and OLDER PEOPLE to "ACT YOUNGER."

Is the purpose of some LEGALESE, CLARITY or SUBTERFUGE?

Everyone will never AGREE on what THE ANSWER or THE SOLUTION IS.

WHO or What WE LOVE, WANT, FEAR, BELIEVE and HOW WE THINK, ultimately DETERMINES HOW WE spiritually "FEEL."

We can sometimes CHANGE OUR FEELINGS, by CHANGING OUR MINDS.

Many SERIOUS THINKERS will have "HOLES" in THEIR LOGIC, and many COMEDIANS will have SOME LOGIC in their LUNACY.

In "THE MALE/FEMALE WARS," there are couples WHO CANNOT GET ALONG but CANNOT LEAVE EACH OTHER ALONE.

Do WE PRAY, because WE FEAR that IF WE DID NOT, GOD WOULD NOT DO THE RIGHT THING?

Why do so many people ask others TO "PRAY FOR THEM," as though, it is better than PRAYING FOR THEMSELVES?

We think that THE MORE PEOPLE WHO PRAY FOR US, THE BETTER. As though GOD is like A POLITICIAN and IS IMPRESSED WITH LARGE NUMBERS.

Some BLACKS and SOME OTHER MINORITIES ENVY and RESENT "WHITE PEOPLE" for THEIR DOMINANCE, THEIR ELITISM, THEIR RACISM, THEIR ADVANTAGES and THEIR PRIVILEGES; otherwise, "THEY LOVE THEM."

# RIGHT CAN BE WRONG

"I'M SORRY — GOD DOESN'T UNDERSTAND U.S. TAX LAWS EITHER."

Some of US are AFRAID to FACE our TRUE SELVES, because OUR TRUE SELVES know THE TRUTH ABOUT US.

We must LEARN TO LIVE WITH OURSELVES, before WE CAN LIVE WELL with OTHERS.

If people DON'T LIKE OUR QUESTIONS, they will QUESTION THEM.

When most people purport TO TELL US HOW TO DO SOMETHING "RIGHT," they are just telling us HOW THEY WOULD DO IT.

Some of those WHO ARE "PART OF THE PROBLEM," BELIEVE THEY ARE MOSTLY "THE SOLUTION."

Most TYRANTS, DESPOTS, DICTATORS and AUTHORITARIANS are "SPIRITUALLY WEAK" PEOPLE; it is A MISNOMER, to call them "STRONGMEN."

For A LIFE TO BE "WELL BALANCED," FAILURES are as much required as SUCCESSES.

We WANT as many FRIENDS as possible, but we "NEED" only ONE "GREAT ONE."

Some of us BUY BIGGER AND BETTER THINGS TO PROVE TO OTHERS that WE ARE BIGGER and BETTER THAN THEM.

IF "GOD DOES NOT GIVE US MORE THAN WE CAN HANDLE," why do some people HAVE PANIC ATTACKS, NERVOUS BREAKDOWNS, GO INSANE or COMMIT SUICIDE?

TRUE, or GENUINE LOVE is never in a hurry TO MARRY, because REAL LOVE CAN WAIT.

We cannot PROTECT OUR CHILDREN from "ALL BAD THINGS"; in fact, it is ultimately A GOOD THING if they experience some of them.

SOME WOMEN believe THAT "ALL MEN ARE DOGS," and SOME MEN believe THAT "ALL WOMEN CAN BE BOUGHT."

ALL MEN ARE NOT DOGS, and ALL WOMEN CANNOT BE BOUGHT --- JUST SOME OF THEM.

In ROMANTIC RELATIONSHIPS, we expect more from THE OTHER than we expect FROM OURSELVES.

There is "AN INVERSE RELATIONSHIP" between THE PHYSICAL and THE SPIRITUAL: The more we have of one, the less we have of the other.

The people who most DETEST receiving "UNSOLICITED ADVICE" tend to be the people MORE LIKELY TO GIVE IT.

Most MEAN and NASTY PEOPLE think, THEY ARE "A GOOD PERSON."

BLACK WOMEN "HOLD" THE BLACK FAMILY, THE BLACK CHURCH and BLACK AMERICA, "TOGETHER."

Can we ERADICATE POVERTY, without ERADICATING WEALTH? Some POOR PEOPLE have created some of the WEALTHY and SOME OF THE WEALTHY PEOPLE have created SOME OF THE POOR.

Do WE want "MOSTLY FREEDOM" or "MOSTLY SECURITY?" WE CANNOT HAVE A LOT OF BOTH.

Sometimes, we wish that we COULD FIGHT OUR CHILDREN'S BATTLES FOR THEM.

Some ROMANTIC LOVE is TOO HOT, and SOME LOGIC is TOO COLD.

The older WE GET, the smarter OUR ELDERS BECOME.

PLEASURE is found OUTSIDE, but JOY is found INSIDE.

Most HEDONISTS or "PLEASURE SEEKERS," LACK JOY.

When MOST PEOPLE are SEEKING THEIR RIGHTS, it is because of SOMETHING THE AUTHORITIES ARE DOING WRONG.

MALE TO MALE FRIENDSHIPS ARE MOSTLY BASED ON MUTUAL INTERESTS. FEMALE TO FEMALE FRIENDSHIPS ARE MOSTLY BASED ON MUTUAL LOYALTY.

QUESTION EVERYTHING and EVERYONE, but most people WILL RESENT YOU FOR IT.

WHATEVER THE EXPERTS SAY TODAY, ANOTHER EXPERT will prove some of them WRONG, TOMORROW.

SOME SERMONS HAVE NO RELEVANCY TO WHAT IS HAPPENING IN "THE REAL WORLD."

Some CONSERVATIVES need to become MORE LIBERAL, and some LIBERALS need to become MORE CONSERVATIVE.

Our LIVES MEAN NOTHING, unless WE MAKE THEM MEAN SOMETHING.

The better ways TODAY to succeed IN POP CULTURE: Do something OUTSTANDING or OUTLANDISH.

*RIGHT CAN BE WRONG*

We either ADAPT or ADJUST to THE WORLD or BECOME LIKE HITLER and try TO GET THE WORLD TO ADAPT or ADJUST TO US.

Living long enough to become A CENTENARIAN is "A GIFT," and not "A SECRET."

We say "LIFE IS SHORT" no matter HOW LONG IT LASTS, because WE NEVER WANT IT TO END.

We either WORRY TOO MUCH, or TOO LITTLE.

FEMALES CRY TOO MUCH, and MALES DON'T CRY ENOUGH.

We can tell what people THINK OF US by the way THEY SPEAK TO US.

MOST OF US, cannot THINK OF GOD, in any other way THAN AS A STRONG and POWERFUL "MALE PERSON."

Do RACISTS BELIEVE that GOD is WHITE?

The next person who asks you, "DO YOU BELIEVE IN GOD?" ask them WHAT Does "THAT WORD" MEAN TO THEM. If they have no answer, they have NO RIGHT to ask THE QUESTION.

Do we really want to BRING ALL THE PEOPLES OF THE WORLD TOGETHER? Do we want everyone to FEEL, BELIEVE and THINK THE SAME?

If you claim YOU DON'T WANT EVERYONE TO FEEL, BELIEVE and THINK the same, THEN THAT IS THE ONLY WAY YOU ARE GOING TO UNITE THE WORLD AS "ONE."

## RIGHT CAN BE WRONG

Some of our POLICE OFFICERS are AFRAID IN THE STREETS. There are only a few things MORE "DANGEROUS" than A FEARFUL POLICE OFFICER.

If some of us suddenly won A BILLION DOLLARS, the first thing WE WOULD BUY, is MORE MONEY PROBLEMS.

We are STRONG, FREE and TRUTH SEEKERS, only when we STOP BELIEVING ALL the "well intentioned" LIES, WE'VE BEEN TAUGHT or TOLD.

Some JOBS do not REQUIRE A LOT OF WORK, and A LOT OF WORK is not always A REAL JOB.

We tend to want MORE CREDIT and LESS BLAME than we deserve.

How do we verbally DESCRIBE A SOUND to A DEAF PERSON, or A COLOR to A BLIND PERSON?

It makes HAPPY PEOPLE "UNHAPPY," when others are not HAPPY TOO.

It makes UNHAPPY PEOPLE "HAPPY" when others are UNHAPPY.

ATTITUDE IS EVERYTHING: It takes the same amount of TIME and ENERGY to do most of what WE LOVE TO DO as it takes to do most of WHAT WE HATE TO DO.

Do the people WHO THANK GOD FOR SAVING THEIR LIVES, believe GOD NEVER WANTS THEM TO DIE?

Some days IT WILL RAIN, sometimes THERE WILL BE PAIN, EVERYTHING WILL ALWAYS CHANGE and NOTHING WILL REMAIN THE SAME; RIGHT will become WRONG, and WRONG will become RIGHT.

LIFE is TOO MUCH for SOME OF US.

PHYSICALLY HEALTHY PEOPLE sometimes THINK THEY ARE SICK, and SPIRITUALLY SICK PEOPLE ALWAYS THINK THEY ARE HEALTHY.

Some DRIVERS are DISCOURTEOUS, because they do not want us TO GET THERE before them, WHEREVER "THERE" IS.

If we had lived IN THE ANCIENT WORLD, relative to today: LIFE WAS VERY SHORT, VERY LIMITED, VERY UNHEALTHY and SCARCELY WORTH LIVING --- but its CITIZENS DID NOT KNOW IT.

Some people do not read GOOD BOOKS, because they are too busy READING "THE GOOD BOOK."

If we have A NEGATIVE HABIT, we try to call it "A DISEASE," because no one can BLAME US for being "SICK."

We cannot always believe SURVEYS and POLLS, because we cannot always believe what people say.

We cannot ALWAYS BELIEVE what WE SAY.

We have NOT LISTENED to "GOOD ADVICE," unless WE FOLLOW IT.

When MOST YOUNG SINGLE ADULTS go out to SOCIAL EVENTS, they are engaging in "MATING GAMES."

Almost ALL "SELF- PRAISE" is QUESTIONABLE or SUSPECT.

PERSONAL PREJUDICE or RACISM is so difficult for the perpetrators TO SEE, because some of it may be "UNCONSCIOUS."

## RIGHT CAN BE WRONG

"AND I HEAR HE EVEN BRUSHES HIS TEETH TEN TIMES A DAY WITH A SOLID GOLD TOOTHBRUSH."

POLYGAMY is having many mates at THE SAME TIME; AMERICAN MONOGAMY is having A DIFFERENT SINGLE MATE, TIME AFTER TIME AFTER TIME.

SOME "LOVING" WHITE PEOPLE feel badly because THEY CANNOT CHANGE their RACIST FAMILY AND FRIENDS.

Some people PUSH US, and PUSH US, just to SEE HOW FAR THEY CAN PUSH US.

PEOPLE who can't "DO IT," ENVY PEOPLE WHO CAN (anything).

Sometimes, In POP CULTURE, "BULLSHIT" SELLS WELL.

What some television TALK SHOWS and GAME SHOWS do best is GIVE AWAY MONEY.

People will SELL, whatever people WILL BUY.

When some people's lips say, "I LOVE YOU," there ACTIONS or BEHAVIOR says OTHERWISE.

KIND PEOPLE are sometimes ABUSED or USED, because THEY ALLOW MORE PUSH, than PUSH BACK.

Like "SPOILED CHILDREN," WE DO NOT CONSIDER OUR PRAYERS ANSWERED, unless WE GET WHAT WE WANT.

For some RELIGIOUS PEOPLE, "PRAYER" is THE ANSWER or THE SOLUTION to EVERYTHING.

How many FOLLOWERS of RICH PREACHERS are AS RICH AS THEM? Do you think that GOD wants you to be RICHLY REWARDED, or that GOD MEANT for THE PREACHERS to be REWARDED RICHLY?

RICH PREACHERS can create more BELIEVERS but cannot CREATE MORE RICH PEOPLE.

Is it MORALLY CORRECT for BUSINESSES or CHURCHES to use their ACTS OF LOVE AND KINDNESS as ADVERTISING FOR NEW BUSINESS or TO RAISE MORE MONEY?

When WE PAY for A PRODUCT or A SERVICE, the PROVIDERS are NOT NECESSARILY "HELPING US."

PROVIDERS would only be "HELPING US," if they PROVIDED FREELY

HELP is ALWAYS either PHYSICAL or SPIRITUAL; we can HELP OTHERS PHYSICALLY, but people can ONLY HELP THEMSELVES SPIRITUALLY. So, we can ONLY HELP PEOPLE HELP THEMSELVES.

Does it ever BOTHER YOU that the things that you consider "TREASURES" are not as POPULAR or AS PROFITABLE as the things that you consider "TRASH?"

Do you believe PEOPLE TODAY can still BE "SAINTS," or are ALL THE TRUE SAINTS DEAD?

Do you BELIEVE that if most people thought they could GET AWAY WITH IT, they would break all THE RULES or LAWS?

Do you think that MOST PEOPLE REALIZE that LAWS or RULES, are LIKE "TRAFFIC LIGHTS," regulating PROPER HUMAN CONDUCT within A CIVILIZED SOCIETY; and that it is in EVERYONE'S BEST INTEREST to ABIDE by THEM? Or do you BELIEVE that ALL OF US are ONLY ALWAYS THINKING ABOUT OURSELVES?

We are ALL IMPERFECT BEINGS, there is something RIGHT and WRONG about all of US – and THAT IS ONE OF OUR MOST SERIOUS PROBLEMS.

If you knew THEN what you know NOW, would you BE what you are NOW, or DO what YOU HAVE DONE?

When WE ARGUE with OURSELVES, it is not ALWAYS WISE to FAVOR OURSELVES.

If we are RIGHT or CORRECT in WHAT WE PRAY FOR, why won't GOD change those things, that we PRAY FOR, so that WE WOULD NOT HAVE TO PRAY FOR THEM?

How many of us SINCERELY BELIEVE that "ULTIMATELY," there is "ONLY ONE RACE?"

ROMANTICS never bother themselves with IMPORTANT DETAILS

The moment you DO SOMETHING to SOMEONE ELSE, that YOU WOULD NOT WANT SOMEONE ELSE to DO TO YOU, you have DONE SOMETHING WRONG.

Some parents would say, "NOTHING RIGHT IS DONE LATE AT NIGHT."

Telling adults, THEY CAN LIVE THEIR "BEST LIVES" WITHOUT MATES is tantamount TO TELLING CHILDREN THEY CAN LIVE THEIR BEST LIVES WITHOUT EDUCATION.

TIME DOES "NOT HEAL ALL THINGS"; ALL THINGS OVER TIME BECOME BETTER or WORST.

If you believe "GOD CREATED US ALL" and that "GOD DOESN'T MAKE MISTAKES," then WHAT ARE "BIRTH DEFECTS?"

*RIGHT CAN BE WRONG*

Some of us THINK WE ARE "A LITTLE NOTHING,' unless we BECOME "A BIG SOMETHING."

The more TIME and EFFORT we devote to "OUR OUTSIDE," the less we tend TO DEVOTE TO "OUR INSIDE."

When we are DETERMINED to SEE SOMETHING GOOD in our ROMANTIC INTEREST, we will not allow ourselves TO SEE ANYTHING ELSE.

Some of what "WE DON'T KNOW" can hurt us, BUT WE WON'T KNOW IT.

VERY SERIOUS PEOPLE think the world is TOO SILLY, and VERY FUNNY PEOPLE think the world is TOO SERIOUS.

HAVING "AN EDUCATED MIND" and "A LARGE LOVING SPIRIT" is more likely TO MAKE US HAPPY than POSSESSING A LOT OF MONEY.

WOMEN respect GENTLENESS, and MEN respect TOUGHNESS.

"There is nothing new under the sun," except CREATIVE IDEAS.

"The truth can set us free," or IT CAN IMPRISON US.

SOME WHITE PEOPLE believe "THEY OWN AMERICA."

GOOD ADVICE does not always HELP US, because we do not ALWAYS RECOGNIZE IT.

Some of the SAME THINGS we like in people WE LIKE; WE DISLIKE in people WE DISLIKE.

We cannot tell some people WHAT THEIR PROBLEM IS, because some people ARE NOT ALWAYS MATURE ENOUGH, to UNDERSTAND WHAT THEIR PROBLEM IS.

TOO LITTLE PRAISE or TOO MUCH PRAISE is PROBLEMATIC.

We cannot give GOOD ADVICE to FOOLISH PEOPLE or STUPID PEOPLE, because they believe GOOD ADVICE is BAD ADVICE.

We do not understand what WE HAVE HEARD or READ, unless we can explain it "IN OTHER WORDS."

BULLIES ARE ATTRACTED to FEAR and WEAKNESS in other people. They do not respect SWEET or NICE; the ONLY WAY to CONFRONT or DEAL WITH A BULLY, is TO BECOME A BULLY TOO.

Many TOUGH or AGGRESSIVE PEOPLE don't know how to be SWEET or NICE, and many SWEET or NICE PEOPLE don't know how to be TOUGH or AGGRESSIVE.

Heterosexuals who believe THAT HOMOSEXUALITY IS "A CHOICE" should ask themselves, AT WHAT POINT IN LIFE DID "THEY CHOOSE" TO BECOME HETEROSEXUAL.

CHILDREN are AFRAID of THE DARK; ADULTS are AFRAID of THE LIGHT

If we share A BED, why is the person WHO SNORES always THE FIRST TO FALL ASLEEP?

Everyone is INTERESTED in HOW THEY LOOK, WHAT OTHERS THINK OF THEM, and IF THEY ARE RESPECTED, LIKED or LOVED.

THE PAST CAN NEVER BE ERASED and THE FUTURE HASN'T BEEN WRITTEN YET.

If OUR NAME has more than TWO SYLLABLES, people will 'REFUSE" to say ALL OF IT.

THE PRESENT and THE FUTURE are always CREATED and PRODUCED by THE PAST.

IN RURAL AREAS, people who live miles apart consider themselves NEIGHBORS, but IN THE BIG CITY, people share the same walls, and DO NOT KNOW ONE ANOTHER --- AND DO NOT WANT TO KNOW ONE ANOTHER.

SMALL TOWN PEOPLE ARE NEIGHBORLY but NOSY; but IN THE BIG CITY, "WE ARE ALL STRANGERS."

The kind of LIES WE TELL reveal THE TRUTH about US.

One of the first things SMALL CHILDREN LEARN is HOW WELL they can control their parents WITH THEIR TEARS.

LIFE is much like A PRIZE FIGHT: We must know HOW TO TAKE A PUNCH, know HOW TO GET UP WHEN KNOCKED DOWN, and we must never allow ourselves TO BE KNOCKED OUT.

We are not willing to ACCEPT A LOT OF EXCUSES FROM OTHERS but WANT OTHERS TO ACCEPT OUR EXCUSES.

Would you rather be THE RICHEST, THE GREATEST, THE MOST HEROIC, THE MOST ATTRACTIVE, THE SAINTLIEST, THE MOST TALENTED, THE MOST FAMOUS, THE WISEST or THE SMARTEST person AMONG US? NO, you cannot be them all.

LIFE is so COMPLEX because WE EXPECT IT TO BE so SIMPLE.

*RIGHT CAN BE WRONG*

"AFTER SEVERAL MILLION YEARS — YOU'D THINK WE WOULD HAVE LEARNED."

Is a BI-RACIAL PERSON still CONSIDERED more BLACK than WHITE? If so, we have accepted "THE ONE DROP RULE."

Because MOST BLACK PEOPLE in AMERICA have SOME WHITE BLOOD, BIRACIAL PEOPLE are "LOGICALLY" WHITER THAN BLACKER, but NOT "CULTURALLY."

LIFE cannot BE EASILY FIGURED OUT, because IT IS TOO LARGE, TOO COMPLEX, TOO IRONIC, TOO CONTRADICTORY and HAS TOO MANY CONUNDRUMS.

We tend to want OUR LOGIC to ALWAYS EQUAL our MORAL BELIEFS, and THEY DO NOT.

How many THINGS or SITUATIONS can you SAY, that are ALWAYS or ABSOLUTELY TRUE?

HUMAN EXISTENCE is NOT AMENABLE to STATIC or STANDARD RULES or LAWS because WE ARE ALWAYS CHANGING. What is RIGHT can become WRONG.

With EVERY NEW GENERATION, "ORGANIZED RELIGION" will LOSE some of ITS POWER or DOMINANCE over THE MASSES; just AS TODAY, it is not AS POWERFUL or DOMINANT, as it was in THE ANCIENT WORLD or THE MIDDLE AGES.

If we must "TAKE THE BITTER with THE SWEET," sometimes if we try to make THE BITTER SWEETER, we will only make THE SWEET, BITTER.

Why do WE HAVE TO PRAY or BEG GOD to "DO THE RIGHT THING?"

The DESIRE FOR WEALTH tends to CREATE "SINNERS" and THE DESIRE TO BE MORE LOVING or KIND tends to CREATE "SAINTS."

Some "FREE THINGS" in LIFE will EVENTUALLY COST US.

Many elderly people WILL NOT SPEND THE MONEY THEY DO HAVE, and many YOUNG PEOPLE WILL SPEND MONEY THEY DON'T HAVE.

MONEY cannot DO EVERYTHING, but ALMOST NOTHING CAN BE DONE WITHOUT IT.

"CROOKED PEOPLE" cannot SEE or THINK STRAIGHT.

IF THE HOLY BOOKS WERE WRITTEN TODAY, do you think ANYONE WOULD PUBLISH, BUY or READ THEM?

Our FAVORITE SUBJECT is "OURSELVES."

Do you think "RELIGION" mostly CAUSES or SOLVES our PROBLEMS?

RACE is "THE ELEPHANT IN THE ROOM," of EVERY IMPORTANT DISCUSSION or THING THAT IS HAPPENING IN AMERICA.

IF WE BELIEVE, we want TO GET TO HEAVEN, but WE DON'T WANT TO DIE.

IF WE DIE and NOTHING ELSE HAPPENS, WE WOULDN'T KNOW IT.

Don't ask people IF THE WORKERS DESERVE HIGHER WAGES. ASK THEM IF THEY WANT TO PAY HIGHER PRICES FOR GOODS and SERVICES.

Some people DON'T MAKE ENOUGH MONEY, no matter HOW MUCH MONEY THEY MAKE.

People WHO BEMOAN the ERADICATION of CONFEDERATE MONUMENTS are only THINKING OF THEMSELVES; THEY FORGET THAT THEY REPRESENT "THE ENSLAVEMENT" OF BLACK PEOPLE.

THE "BEST" or THE "MOST RIGHTEOUS" DOES NOT ALWAYS WIN.

THE LAW initially "PRESUMES" THAT EVERYONE IS INNOCENT, but NO ONE ELSE DOES.

IF we become RICH and/or FAMOUS, more people WILL LIKE US and MORE PEOPLE WILL DISLIKE US.

We ENTER LIFE, "LOST"; we must live life SEARCHING FOR OURSELVES.

GENUINE "LOVE" is not ALWAYS LOVELY, SWEET or NICE.

We do not need BIGGER and BETTER THINGS to BE HAPPY, but we do if WE WANT PEOPLE TO BELIEVE WE ARE "THE HAPPIEST."

When we MAKE PREDICTIONS, WE EITHER PREDICT OUR WISHES or OUR FEARS.

ALL ROMANTIC RELATIONSHIPS will EVENTUALLY BECOME MORE LOVING or CREATE GREATER DISLIKES.

*RIGHT CAN BE WRONG*

Some people WANT THE PROMOTION, but DON'T WANT THE JOB.
ALL FEAR IS ROOTED IN THE FEAR OF DEATH.

BELIEFS or OPINIONS are WHAT WE FEEL. FACTS, TRUTHS, SCIENCE and KNOWLEDGE are WHAT WE CAN LOGICALLY EXPLAIN or PHYSICALLY DEMONSTRATE.

If we cannot do anything about WORLD EVENTS, we enjoy talking about WHAT SHOULD BE DONE.

We tend TO EXPECT HAPPINESS or SUCCESS before WE KNOW PRECISELY WHAT THEY MEAN.

When we are young, we are mostly INFLUENCED, MOTIVATED or DRIVEN by IMPULSES that WE DO NOT ALWAYS UNDERSTAND.

We NEED TRAINING or A LICENSE to DRIVE A CAR, but almost ANYONE CAN RAISE A HUMAN BEING. In THE FUTURE, this must be DEALT WITH.

Many WOMEN believe, THEY ARE ONLY WORTH WHAT THEY LOOK LIKE.

People in THE FIRST WORLD are NOT BETTER than those IN THE THIRD WORLD, just "BETTER OFF."

We should not just be assessed BY HOW FAR WE GO IN LIFE, but also, BY HOW FAR WE'VE COME. When the child of A POOR PERSON becomes PRESIDENT, it is MORE IMPRESSIVE than WHEN THE CHILD OF A RICH PERSON BECOMES PRESIDENT.

Some of us WILL "FIND OURSELVES," and SOME OF US WILL DIE SEARCHING.

We keep COMPARING AMERICA TO OTHER COUNTRIES, when we know THERE IS NO OTHER COUNTRY IN THE WORLD THAT AMERICA CAN BE PRECISELY COMPARED TO.

There are NEGATIVE and POSITIVE TRUTHS, and there are NEGATIVE and POSITIVE LIES.

The MOST POWERFUL PEOPLE in BLACK AMERICA, have always been "THE PREACHERS."

Nearly EVERYONE claims they know HOW PROBLEMS SHOULD BE SOLVED, but ONLY A FEW are willing to TRY TO SOLVE THEM.

What HUMANS most WANT TO DO IN LIFE, is "LIVE."

IN THIS LIFE, one cannot SEE ANY SIGNIFICANCE DIFFERENCE in the lives OF RELIGIOUS BELIEVERS and THE LIVES of NON-BELIEVERS.

There is NO DOUBT that some RELIGIOUS BELIEVERS NO LONGER BELIEVE, but THEY ARE AFRAID to "CONFESS."

Some of us WANT OUR ENTERTAINMENT or AMUSEMENTS to DISTRACT US from FACING OURSELVES.

POP CULTURE is A WORLD OF "MAKE BELIEVE."

Almost NO ONE "TURNS THE OTHER CHEEK." We see it AS DEFEAT or BEING WEAK.

When WE DON'T KNOW WHAT SHOULD BE DONE, DOING A LITTLE, WILL BE SEEN AS HAVING DONE A LOT.

Does PRAYER CHANGE "THINGS" or does PRAYER CHANGE PEOPLE?

PRAYERS are what we do WHEN WE DON'T KNOW WHAT ELSE TO DO.

Becoming "A SAINT" is "TOO HARD," so some of us settle FOR READING THE HOLY BOOKS and ATTENDING RELIGIOUS SERVICES REGULARLY.

When WE CANNOT CONTROL OURSELVES, we derive GREAT SATISFACTION IN CONTROLLING OTHERS.

One of THE MOST UNFAIR THINGS in our UNFAIR EXISTENCE, is the fact THAT WHATEVER TAKES A LIFETIME TO BUILD, can be DESTROYED IN "AN INSTANT."

Do you think that THIS "MAN'S WORLD" will ever BECOME "A WOMAN'S WORLD?"

Some "HUMAN TREASURES" are NEVER DISCOVERED.

Some of us LIKE SAINTS and ANGELS, and some of us LIKE SINNERS and EARTHLY DEVILS.

A large problem with LIFE IN GENERAL is that THE PEOPLE IN CONTROL are NOT ALWAYS THE BEST PEOPLE TO BE IN CONTROL.

IF "BEAUTY IS IN THE EYE OF THE BEHOLDER," then some BEHOLDERS ARE "BLIND."

MANY LIVES are SIMILAR, but NO LIFE is PRECISELY LIKE any other.

A HIGHLY EDUCATED PERSON cannot EXPECT A POORLY EDUCATED PERSON to MOSTLY UNDERSTAND THEM.

*RIGHT CAN BE WRONG*

THE LANDINGS are always HARSH or ROUGH for THOSE WHO HAVE FLOWN "TOO HIGH."

Some SINS are not CRIMES, and some CRIMES are NOT SINS.

Believe it or not, SOME CHURCHES and RELIGIONS, TELL LIES TOO.

Many people would rather LOOK STUPID or IGNORANT, rather than ADMIT BEING WRONG.

We either MOSTLY WANT TO BE AMUSED OR ENTERTAINED, or MOSTLY ENLIGHTENED OR EDUCATED.

RELIGION cannot be LOGICALLY DEDUCED and SCIENCE cannot be EMOTIONALLY SENSED.

We use PRETTY LIES to REPLACE UGLY TRUTHS.

We are MOSTLY responsible for CREATING OUR OWN PROBLEMS; but WE MOSTLY BLAME OTHERS.

Anything we WRITE or SAY, "MAY BE USED AGAINST US."

It is so difficult to become BIGGER and BETTER, because the first step for some of us IS TO ADMIT THAT WE ARE NOT THAT ALREADY.

Those of us WHO ENJOY SEEING "A GOOD FIGHT," do not care what the fight is about.

In SOME CULTURES, or COUNTRIES, what ONCE WAS RIGHT is NOW WRONG.

We are RAISING OUR YOUNG to believe THAT THE GREATEST THING TO BE is to be RICH and FAMOUS.

## RIGHT CAN BE WRONG

MOST OF US just WANT TO LOOK GOOD, FEEL GOOD, BE RICH, BE FAMOUS, WIN and BE RIGHT.

Some RELIGIOUS SPEAKERS believe that the more "EMOTIONALLY CHARGED" their SERMONS ARE, the more their LISTENERS WILL BELIEVE THEM. Or perhaps THE MORE THEY WILL "FEEL THEM."

Some POOR PEOPLE cannot AFFORD TO PAY FOR JUSTICE.

ANOTHER DEFINITION OF "HAPPINESS": Instead of GETTING WHAT WE WANT, "WANTING WHAT WE GET."

We can BE "BROKE" without BEING BROKEN.

THE WORSE POOR PEOPLE SUFFER, THE WORST SOME RICH PEOPLE FEEL.

The foods THAT WE LIKE, do not always LIKE US.

Some CORRECT GRAMMAR does not SOUND RIGHT, and SOME INCORRECT GRAMMAR DOES.

IN PUBLIC, we are mostly POSING, PERFORMING, PRETENDING or POSTURING.

We love OUR PET ANIMALS SO MUCH, because they are the only BEINGS, WE CAN SHARE LOVE WITH and STILL BE IN TOTAL CONTROL.

THE HOLY BOOKS had to have been written SIMPLY, because most of the people in THE ANCIENT WORLD could not READ or WRITE.

Are RELIGIOUS PROSELYTIZERS trying to CONVINCE US or THEMSELVES.

Do you ever WONDER how many things TELEVISION HOSTS PRETEND TO LIKE, THAT THEY DON'T LIKE.

MOST PEOPLE cannot THINK in any other way other than IN HUMAN or PHYSICAL WAYS; that is why GOD is described IN SUCH HUMAN or PHYSICAL TERMS.

The MORE WE LEARN, the more WE REALIZE how much WE DO NOT KNOW.

The "RED BLACKLISTS" in the "FIFTIES" were a way for WHITE PEOPLE to know what RACISM is like FOR SOME BLACK PEOPLE, EVERYDAY.

A THEORY ON HOARDERS: When we feel we have nothing in our lives of any REAL or GREAT VALUE, then EVERYTHING IN OUR LIVES CAN HAVE VALUE.

What does it SAY ABOUT US when we would rather hear THE NASTY, more THAN THE NICE?

MALES who accuse FEMALES of being "GOLD DIGGERS" because they will not give them FREE SEX, are AS CORRUPT as THE ACCUSED.

PROFUSE SPOKEN PROFANITIES are the manifestations of A WEAK VOCABULARY.

We are NEVER RACIST or PREJUDICED in OUR SEXUAL BEHAVIOR.

We cannot SURVIVE very long in any SOCIAL ORDER without sometimes "GOING ALONG TO GET ALONG."

Some NON-BELIEVERS put on THE CLOAK OF GOD, to SCAM THE BELIEVERS.

*RIGHT CAN BE WRONG*

Being A LARGE "SOMEBODY" can be as STRESSFUL as being "A NOBODY."

LOVE asks US to CONSIDER or CARE for "ALL SIDES," but LIFE forces us to "TAKE SIDES."

When BLACK PEOPLE practice COLORISM among one another, they are doing the same thing to themselves, that RACIST WHITE PEOPLE have been doing to them for HUNDREDS OF YEARS.

When WE FOCUS ON "THE BIG PICTURE," the smaller things matter less.

We cannot always SEE OURSELVES, by OURSELVES.

THE BETTER PART of living A FALLIBLE EXISTENCE is that MOST THINGS that BREAKDOWN or GO WRONG, can BE FIXED or MADE RIGHT.

ONLY When WE REALIZE or ACCEPT that WE ALL are "ALONE" IN THE WORLD, can we GET ALONG BETTER WITH OTHERS.

Even if we have GREAT DEFINITIONS for ABSTRACT TERMS like GOD, HEAVEN, HELL and HAPPINESS, not EVERYONE WILL AGREE.

HAPPINESS is and is not A CONSTANT STATE and is RELATIVE to other STATES of BEING. ABSTRACT CONCEPTS are CONSTANTLY CHANGING, and once WE CALL THEM ONE THING, THEY can BECOME SOMETHING ELSE. We cannot FOCUS ON THE WORDS, because THE WORDS are FOCUSED ON US. And WE ARE CONSTANTLY CHANGING.

Even if you did KNOW SOME OF "THE ANSWERS," or "SOLUTIONS," there is NO GUARANTEE that ANYONE WOULD LISTEN TO YOU.

We are probably already LOOKING AT "THE NEXT BIG THING"; we just CAN'T SEE IT.

Does EVERYONE have THE RIGHT to DEFINE or INTERPRET LOVE and GOD ANYWAY they wish?

We get NOTHING for NOTHING.

In order TO GET ALONG WITH NEARLY EVERYONE, we must know HOW CLOSE to ALLOW PEOPLE TO APPROACH US.

Most of us want to reach "THE TOP OF THE MOUNTAIN," without doing a lot of "CLIMBING."

It is FUTILE to tell PROBLEM GAMBLERS that "THE ODDS ARE AGAINST THEM," because THOSE ARE THE ODDS that they are determined "TO BEAT."

ACCIDENTS never COSTS what WE CAN AFFORD.

Almost EVERY CELEBRITY is PLAYING A ROLE in REAL LIFE, and SOME are "MASTERS OF DECEIT."

EVERYONE "LOVES A WINNER," except WHEN THEY WIN TOO MUCH or TOO OFTEN.

We are all HONEST and DISHONEST to VARYING DEGREES.

We can LOVE HUMANITY at a distance, but WE CANNOT LOVE INDIVIDUALS THAT WAY.

After "A CERTAIN AGE," every move we make is GREAT EXERCISE.

Many WOMEN and MOST CHILDREN do not tell us WHAT THEY THINK – they TELL US WHAT THEY FEEL.

After "A CERTAIN AGE" Some of us decide that WE UNDERSTAND LIFE, and DON'T NEED TO LEARN ANYMORE ABOUT IT.

There are SOME THINGS we won't BE SERIOUS ABOUT, but ALMOST NOTHING we won't JOKE ABOUT.

Have we EVER SEEN an ATHLETE WIN an ARGUMENT with AN UMPIRE or REFEREE?

Is it BETTER to "FALL IN LOVE" or GROW IN LOVE?

BABIES SLEEP SO MUCH and SO WELL, because THEY HAVE ABSOLUTELY NOTHING ON THEIR MINDS: WE ADULTS CAN GET A GOOD NIGHT'S SLEEP TOO, if "WE DON'T PUT OUR MINDS TO IT."

Some AMERICANS spend MONEY THEY DON'T HAVE, to buy THINGS THEY DON'T REALLY WANT, THEY DON'T NEED and CANNOT AFFORD.

TRUTH IS STRANGER THAN FICTION because TRUTH does not ALWAYS SOUND or FEEL TRUTHFUL.

We only want to HEAR OPINIONS we AGREE WITH.

Is GOD, ALWAYS whatever THE PREACHERS or RELIGIOUS LEADERS say GOD IS?

*RIGHT CAN BE WRONG*

What "QUALIFIES" ANYONE to KNOW ANYMORE about GOD THAN ANYONE ELSE?

GREAT or IMPRESSIVE PEOPLE are RARELY viewed that way AT HOME.

Do you ever wonder IF COUNSELORS ever NEED COUNSELING or if THERAPISTS ever NEED THERAPY?

SOMEONE ELSE in the world always HAS OUR NAME.

IT IS not always "WHAT IT IS," sometimes, IT IS WHAT WE MAKE IT.

We tend to BELIEVE that "WRONG," is ANYONE who is NOT LIVING, BELIEVING or THINKING the same AS US.

Most of us "JUST ACCEPT" what we have been RELIGIOUSLY TOLD or TAUGHT without ANY SERIOUS THOUGHT ABOUT IT. Is it because WE ARE AFRAID TO?

Some AMERICANS still CANNOT SEE, how "SLAVERY" CHANGED AMERICA, FOREVER.

Does SUICIDE mean THAT SOME find LIFE, worse THAN DEATH?

We can TEACH OUR CHILDREN THINGS without REALIZING WHAT WE HAVE TAUGHT and THEY CAN LEARN THINGS, without REALIZING WHAT THEY HAVE LEARNED.

Do you think EVERYONE needs SOMETHING to WORK FOR besides MONEY?

EVERYONE WANTS to "SAVE THE WORLD," THEIR OWN WAY, and this is PRECISELY WHY THE WORLD IS SO DANGEROUS.

Do you think TOO MANY OF OUR LEADERS BEHAVE LIKE CHILDREN?

INFANTS and SMALL CHILDREN are THE MOST AMAZING, because THEY LEARN A LANGUAGE without having "A FRAME OF REFERENCE."

LIFE IS sometimes "TOUGH" FOR EVERYONE, and THAT INCLUDES THE RICH, THE FAMOUS and THE POWERFUL; but IT IS FALLACIOUS to say, THAT LIFE IN GENERAL IS HARD, because there is NOTHING to COMPARE IT TO.

If THE PHYSICAL and THE SPIRITUAL are "MUTUALLY EXCLUSIVE," and FIRE is A PHYSICAL THING, and HELL is A SPIRITUAL PLACE, then HOW CAN THERE BE FIRE IN HELL?

Some WHITE PEOPLE can "SEPARATE" CIVIL WAR HEROES from THE INSTITUTION OF SLAVERY, but BLACK PEOPLE CANNOT.

If we could "LOVE OUR ENEMIES" would that STOP THEM FROM TRYING TO DESTROY US?

Do you BELIEVE that EVERYONE WHO MARRIES, is SOMEONE GOD HAS "PUT TOGETHER?"

If ALL MARRIAGES are people WHOM GOD HAS "PUT TOGETHER," WHY ARE THEIR SO MANY DIVORCES?

If a GOOD or GREAT BOOK is NOT "A BEST SELLER," isn't THAT the PUBLIC'S LOSS?

It took A CIVIL WAR to SEPARATE BLACKS and WHITES in AMERICA; will it TAKE A SOCIAL REVOLUTION to RE-UNITE THEM?

Those who say THEY WILL BE HAPPY WHEN THEY ATTAIN SOMETHING, are treating HAPPINESS AS "A DESTINATION," RATHER THAN "A JOURNEY."

"WAR" is THE MOST INHUMANE THING that HUMANS CAN DO.

It is EASY TO SAY, "WHAT MUST BE DONE" or" WHAT SHOULD BE DONE," IF we don't HAVE TO PERSONALLY DO IT.

We BREAK OUR BACKS to EARN A FORTUNE, but all we can ULTIMATELY do with it, IS GIVE MOST OF IT AWAY.

After many people have ATTAINED A FORTUNE, the numbers ARE JUST THE WAY, "WE KEEP SCORE."

"RIGHT CAN BE WRONG," because OVER TIME things can REVERSE THEMSELVES as WE HUMANS become BIGGER and BETTER. And some formerly "WRONG THINGS BECOME ALL RIGHT."

It is INTERESTING and IRONIC how YOUNG LOVERS TRUST EACH OTHER AFTER KNOWING ONE ANOTHER FOR A VERY SHORT TIME, and DISTRUST THEIR FAMILY or RELATIVES, who have known them ALL OF THEIR LIVES.

We are not WINNERS, unless we are GOOD LOSERS.

MONOTHEISM decided to STREAMLINE or CONSOLIDATE ORGANIZED RELIGION and PUT ALL OF THE POWER IN THE HANDS OF "ONE GOD," instead of leaving it THE HANDS OF MANY GODS(POLYTHEISM).

HISTORICALLY, all OUR "gods" and "SPACE ALIENS" have BEEN "PATTERNED" after WE HUMANS.

## RIGHT CAN BE WRONG

When POLITICIANS do WHAT IS RIGHT, someone will always FEEL that THEY HAVE BEEN DONE WRONG.

Some PEOPLE are TREATED LIKE DOGS, and SOME DOGS are TREATED LIKE PEOPLE.

Some people who pay no special attention to their health LIVE LONGER THAN "THE HEALTH NUTS."

SOMETHING THAT MOST PEOPLE DO NOT BELIEVE: It is SAFER to FLY COMMERCIAL, than it is to RIDE IN A CAR.

About 35,000 people die in CAR ACCIDENTS each year in AMERICA, and a small fraction of that in COMMERCIAL AIR FLIGHTS, yet almost no one SUFFERS FROM "FEAR OF DRIVING" or "FEAR OF RIDING IN A CAR."

Why are MOSTLY WOMEN so AFRAID of BUGS or SMALL CRITTERS?

Most of OUR "FEARS" are ILLOGICAL or DON'T MAKE SENSE.

We always WANT what someone else HAS, and SOMEONE else always wants what WE HAVE.

We want OTHER PEOPLE to WANT WHAT WE HAVE, but not so much as to STEAL FROM US.

One of THE MOST IMPORTANT THINGS WE CAN DO IN LIFE, is decide WHAT ARE THE MOST IMPORTANT THINGS WE CAN DO IN LIFE.

ATHLETES make more money THAN TEACHERS, because MOST PARENTS would rather ATTEND A BALL GAME, than A PARENTS/TEACHERS CONFERENCE.

When people EXPRESS THEIR OPINIONS, do we LEARN MORE about THE PEOPLE or THEIR OPINIONS?

Are PEOPLE mostly THEIR OPINIONS?

YOUNG PEOPLE who PASS OUT when meeting CELEBRITIES need to "WAKE-UP."

We won't allow our children to be "THEMSELVES," because we want our children to be "US."

SOME THINGS that are simultaneously "GOOD" and "BAD": FIRE, WATER, FOOD, RELIGION, SEX and LIFE.

SMALL CHILDREN mostly FEAR WHAT THEIR PARENTS FEAR.

If we are NOT GROWING, we are SHRINKING.

The DANGER ZONE is "EVERYWHERE."

Do you wish TELEVISION HOSTS would stop PUSHING ROMANTICS to SHOW AFFECTION on CAMERA, because IT MAKES THEM and THEIR AUDIENCES FEEL GOOD?

AFFECTION that is PROMPTED or FORCED, never FEELS TRUE or GENUINE.

GOD and LOVE mostly EXISTS "INSIDE OF US."

WHATEVER is INSIDE OF US, we "PROJECT" OUTSIDE OF US.

Regardless of their RACE or ETHNICITY, MOST NON-WHITE PEOPLE who become RICH and FAMOUS become "CULTURALLY WHITE" in AMERICA.

MOST OF US only SHOW COMPASSION for THE POOR or DISADVANTAGED, at CHRISTMAS TIME.

POLITICIANS don't HAVE TO KNOW what SOLVES PROBLEMS; They just must know WHAT MOST PEOPLE BELIEVE WILL SOLVE PROBLEMS, so they can PRETEND to BELIEVE THE SAME.

We always believe that PARENTING IS SOMETHING WE CAN DO, until we realize THAT IT IS NOT; and WE MUST HAVE CHILDREN, to FIND OUT.

We never know "WHAT GOES ON BEHIND CLOSED DOORS," but that doesn't stop us from TRYING TO FIND OUT.

If SOME OF US cannot become FAMOUS, we are willing TO BECOME INFAMOUS.

SOME MEN can assist SOME WOMEN in becoming TOUGH or AGGRESSIVE, and SOME WOMEN can assist SOME MEN in becoming SWEETER, NICER or MORE CIVILIZED.

SCIENCE is based ON LOGIC; RELIGION is based ON LOVE.

LOGIC always MAKES SENSE; LOVE does not always MAKE SENSE but tries TO CARE FOR OTHERS ANYWAY.

LOGIC must TEMPER LOVE, and LOVE MUST SOFTEN LOGIC.

WE STRUGGLE to BALANCE "LOGIC" and "LOVE."

The "TRUTH" can be VERY UNKIND or EVEN CRUEL, and "LIES" CAN BE VERY COMFORTING.

*RIGHT CAN BE WRONG*

We STRUGGLE to BALANCE "BITTER TRUTHS" and "SWEET LIES."

Some people WOULD PREFER that we LISTEN TO THEM, rather than OUR CONSCIENCE.

MOST ARGUMENTS are caused BECAUSE OTHER PEOPLE WILL NOT DO or BE what we want them TO DO or BE.

Very THOUGHTFUL PEOPLE are accused of NOT BEING EMOTIONALLY SENSITIVE, and EMOTIONALLY SENSITIVE PEOPLE are accused of NOT THINKING THINGS THROUGH.

WITH "AI" THE EYES can LIE.

Doesn't "ETERNAL FIRE AND DAMNATION" sounds like "CRUEL AND UNUSUAL PUNISHMENT?"

BLACK young criminals "NEED TO BE THROWN IN JAIL," but WHITE young criminals, "NEED HELP."

It is only NOW do we realize what we should have done or said THEN.

We are all MOSTLY SEEKING SEX, FOOD, MONEY, POWER or GLORY.

All "POWER" seeks TO LEAD, INSTRUCT, DOMINATE or CONTROL OTHERS.

POWER and AUTHORITY seek TO CONTROL or DOMINATE, but FAME and GLORY seek TO BE ADORED or WORSHIPED.

The HARDEST people TO SPEAK OUR TRUTH TO, are THOSE WHOM WE LOVE THE MOST. WE fear that it will diminish or fracture THE RELATIONSHIP.

We are NOT RESPONSIBLE for HOW WE WERE BORN, but THE WORLD won't STOP BLAMING US.

Have you EVER SEEN A BLACK COUPLE or FAMILY, ADOPT A WHITE CHILD?

We tend TO "CORRUPT" THE INTENTIONS OF NATURE: MALES are mostly obsessed with the part of THE FEMALE ANATOMY that nature meant TO SUCKLE THE YOUNG, and the part NATURE MEANT as a cushion FOR SITTING.

We ALWAYS want to DO MORE, than we will EVER BE ABLE TO DO.

RICH and FAMOUS people are always trying to "SELL" others on how they CAN BE LIKE THEM, when THEY ARE THE ONLY PEOPLE WHO CAN BE LIKE THEM.

TWO OF THE HARDEST THINGS TO KNOW: When to SPEAK UP and when to SHUT DOWN.

We are MEASURED by THE AMOUNT of MONEY we CAN MAKE or CAN GENERATE.

THE MOST DIFFICULT BUSINESSES TO BE IN: Any BUSINESS that deals with THE PUBLIC'S CHILDREN, MONEY or PHYSICAL APPEARANCE.

People who DO NOT NEED PERSONAL ADVICE are always READING IT, and PEOPLE WHO don't NEED MUCH EXERCISE are ALWAYS "WORKING OUT."

One of the hardest things to do IS TO LIVE WELL WITH SOMEONE IN THE SAME LIVING SPACE: We cannot necessarily live WELL with someone JUST BECAUSE WE LIKE THEM or THEY ARE OUR FRIENDS.

LIFE is BEAUTIFUL and UGLY. LIFE is HEAVEN and HELL.

Why do we always believe THAT OUR BASIC PRINCIPLES SHOULD NEVER CHANGE?

Are there more GOOD PEOPLE than BAD PEOPLE? The REAL QUESTION IS, are we ALL DOING GOOD or DOING BAD. Because WE ALL are both GOOD and BAD PEOPLE.

THE CHILDREN of THE GREAT, THE HEROIC, THE FAMOUS, or THE SAINTLY PEOPLE have A TREMENDOUS BURDEN PLACED ON THEIR SHOULDERS. People expect them to be LIKE THEIR PARENTS.

Without THEIR HOLY BOOKS and PREACHING, some religious people WOULD NOT KNOW WHAT TO DO.

It never benefits us to be MEAN or NASTY, but it does sometimes, to be TOUGH or AGGRESSIVE.

EGO-MANIACS do not THINK MUCH OF THEMSELVES, which is why THEY MUST PROVE TO THEMSELVES and THE WORLD that THEY ARE THE BIGGEST, THE BEST and THE BRIGHTEST.

We cannot CHANGE THE LARGER WORLD, but when THE LARGER WORLD CHANGES, we must be willing to CHANGE TOO.

Almost NO ONE lives "A BALANCED LIFE": We either THINK TOO LITTLE OF OURSELVES or TOO MUCH.

We DO NOT LIKE PEOPLE who have TOO LITTLE CONFIDENCE and PEOPLE WHO HAVE TOO MUCH.

*RIGHT CAN BE WRONG*

Some of OUR PARENTS cannot PROPERLY LOVE US, because no one has ever PROPERLY LOVED THEM.

Some PRECOCIOUS CHILDREN can SEE CLEARER than THEIR PARENTS and TEACHERS.

Once we BECOME FAMOUS, we can NEVER STOP BEING FAMOUS.

AUTHORITARIANS think THEY HAVE A RIGHT to DO WRONG.

Some FORTUNES are FORTUITOUS.

People MOSTLY TELL US WHAT THEY WANT US TO KNOW ABOUT THEM; but WE MOSTLY WANT TO KNOW WHAT THEY DON'T WANT TO TELL US.

"WHEN ALL IS SAID AND DONE," MORE WILL ALWAYS BE SAID, THAN DONE.

If the law says THAT "EVERYONE IS INNOCENT UNTIL PROVEN GUILTY," what do we do when some CRIMINALS WHO COMMIT CRIMES AGAINST "BLACK PEOPLE" ARE PROVEN TO BE GUILTY, but ARE STILL DECLARED INNOCENT?

We can rarely SEE LIFE or THE WORLD OBJECTIVELY: We mostly see through THE LENS OF OUR OWN LIFE and EXPERIENCES.

GREAT MARRIAGES do not REQUIRE A LOT OF WORK, only NOT GREAT MARRIAGES DO.

Why is BLACK HISTORY MONTH, the month WITH THE FEWEST DAYS?

STATISTICS, FIGURES or NUMBERS cannot ALWAYS BE COUNTED ON.

Our RELIGIOSITY will only BE AS MATURE AS WE ARE.

Many things that BEGIN BEING TOUGH, will eventually BECOME EASIER; and MANY THINGS THAT BEGIN BEING EASY, will eventually BECOME TOUGHER.

We cannot always "GET ON TOP OF THINGS," until "WE HAVE GOTTEN TO THE BOTTOM OF THINGS."

Some "CLICHES" are WORTH REPEATING.

Not ALL RICH and FAMOUS PEOPLE are "SOMETHING SPECIAL"; some are just "SOMETHING LUCKY."

We NEVER know "THE PRICE" someone HAS PAID for THEIR FORTUNE.

How can SEX BEFORE MARRIAGE be "WRONG," if there was SEX BEFORE THERE WAS MARRIAGE?

When HIGH TECH MACHINES START DOING ALL OUR WORK, WHO WILL BUY THE PRODUCTS?

Many people claim to HAVE AN IDEA for an IDEAL or PERFECT FORM OF "GOVERNANCE," but AN IDEAL or PERFECT FORM OF GOVERNANCE NEVER APPEARS.

Can you REMEMBER HOW GOOD YOUR MEMORY IS?

If "GOD IS LOVE," why does GOD HAVE TO BE "A PERSON," but LOVE DOESN'T HAVE TO BE A PERSON?

If "GOD IS LOVE," why do we think GOD is OUTSIDE OF US, but LOVE IS INSIDE OF US?

Have we PROJECTED GOD to be OUTSIDE OF OURSELVES?

SOME FACIAL EXPRESSIONS and BODY LANGUAGES speak LOUDER THAN WORDS.

MESSAGE TO ROMANTICS: Maybe you CAN'T FIND WHAT YOU ARE LOOKING FOR because WHAT YOU ARE LOOKING FOR is NOT LOOKING FOR YOU.

Always LOOK BEYOND THE OUTSIDE, and BELOW THE SURFACE.

FIRST IMPRESSIONS SHOULD NOT BE "LASTING IMPRESSIONS," because ALMOST NOTHING and NO ONE are AS THEY FIRST APPEAR, they are BETTER or WORSE.

Perhaps FIRST IMPRESSIONS ARE JUST SUCCESSFUL ATTEMPTS TO DECEIVE or IMPRESS US.

Maybe WE CANNOT FIND WHAT WE ARE LOOKING FOR, because IT DOES NOT EXIST.

MANY THINGS are "TAKEN FOR GRANTED," until THEY are NO LONGER GRANTED.

Some "GOOD THINGS" are BAD FOR US, and SOME "BAD THINGS" are GOOD FOR US.

American's DESIRES ARE CONTRADICTORY: They want maximum FREEDOM and SECURITY. There is an inverse relationship between FREEDOM and SECURITY: The more we have of one, the less we have of the other. INSECURITY IS PRICE WE PAY FOR SO MUCH FREEDOM.

We must WORK HARD to BE HAPPY, but SADNESS REQUIRES NO EFFORT.

## RIGHT CAN BE WRONG

"OH MABEL, DON'T SLASH YOUR WRIST — I'VE GOT NEW CARPETING IN THERE!"

SOMETIMES, we are not the ONES WHO ARE "WRONG" --- it is EVERYONE ELSE.

It is NEVER GOOD to accuse anyone of DOING ANYTHING BAD.

What else should ROMANTIC RELATIONSHIPS be BASED ON other than GOOD LOOKS, MONEY and SEX?

The things THAT MOST MATTERS in LIFE, are GOOD SPIRITUAL and PHYSICAL HEALTH; everything else IS SECONDARY.

Many People who think THEIR RELIGION IS "THE BEST" have never STUDIED, EXAMINED or EXPERIENCED ANY OTHER.

Some people do not LIKE CHANGE, because it makes them feel UNCOMFORTABLE; they don't realize that it is ONLY WHEN WE ARE UNCOMFORTABLE are we MOTIVATED TO CHANGE THINGS.

EVERYONE has "ANSWERS," but FEW PEOPLE have ANY REAL SOLUTIONS.

WHITE PEOPLE who appear to be concerned about exposing their children TO PAST SLAVERY, seem to have NO COMPUNCTIONS about EXPOSING THEM TO THEIR PRESENT- DAY RACISM and DISCRIMINATION.

YOUNG FEMALES are always concerned about HOW THEY LOOK, and YOUNG MALES are always THINKING ABOUT SEX.

If it is BETTER to be "A SAINT," why are "SINNERS" so much MORE INTERESTING?

Perhaps SAINTS seem SO BORING, because SINNERS seem TO BE HAVING SO MUCH FUN.

When MARRIAGE FAILS, we return TO OUR CHILDHOOD STATE, and FIGHT OVER "THE TOYS."

We cannot BE "WHOLE PERSONS," until we are willing to adopt some of POSITIVE QUALITIES or ASPECTS of THE OPPOSITE GENDER.

MEN can never BE RICH ENOUGH, and FEMALES can NEVER LOOK GOOD ENOUGH.

We are all "PLAYING ROLES," and very few of us are PORTRAYING OURSELVES.

We are ALL DIFFERENT PEOPLE to DIFFERENT PEOPLE.

Just because WE ARE ALL HERE, does not necessarily mean "WE ARE ALL THERE."

If WE HAVE THE RIGHT TO "FREE SPEECH," does that include RACIST, ANTI-SEMITIC, SEXIST, AGIST HOMOPHOBIC, ISLAMOPHOBIC and PROFANE REMARKS?

We are willing TO EAT SOME ANIMALS, and SOME ANIMALS are willing TO EAT US.

People WHO MEAN to "LIVE HIGH," tend TO LIVE HIGHER THAN THEIR MEANS.

It is BAD JUDGMENT for some of us to think that we have GOOD JUDGMENT.

POLITICIANS can never DELIVER EVERYTHING THEY PROMISE.

People are SAYING THE SAME THINGS ABOUT US behind our backs THAT WE ARE SAYING ABOUT THEM.

"ENOUGH IS NOT ENOUGH," WE ALWAYS WANT MORE.

We tend to believe THAT PEOPLE NEED TO KNOW US IN ORDER TO CRITICIZE US, but WE DON'T, in order TO CRITICIZE THEM.

In some MARRIAGES, we do not WANT TO STAY, but DO NOT KNOW HOW TO LEAVE.

If ALL BABIES or INFANTS "GO TO HEAVEN," would it not BEHOOVE US TO DIE VERY YOUNG?

As we seek to MOLD OUR CHILDREN, RAISING OUR CHILDREN WILL BE MOLDING US.

One of the MOST IMPORTANT THINGS IN LIFE to decide is WHAT ARE THE MOST IMPORTANT THINGS IN LIFE.

We cannot ALWAYS get PEOPLE TO DO THE RIGHT THINGS, by TELLING THEM THE RIGHT THINGS TO DO.

WHAT IS OUR POINT, when WE "EXCHANGE" GIFTS at CHRISTMAS TIME? A GIFT is only A GIFT, if we EXPECT NOTHING in RETURN.

HAIR TODAY/GONE TOMORROW.

We can only KNOW SO MUCH, but we can BELIEVE ANYTHING.

SOME SUCCESSFUL PEOPLE do not want to "HELP ANYONE" to REACH THEIR LEVEL of SUCCESS.

Can it be that some actors DO NOT KNOW WHO THEY ARE, because they PRETEND TO BE so MANY DIFFERENT PEOPLE?

How can WHITE PEOPLE call A PEOPLE "LAZY," who BUILT SO MUCH of THE COUNTRY?

*RIGHT CAN BE WRONG*

BITTER TRUTHS are best served with "A DASH," of HUMOR.

Everything "RIGHT" in A FREE COUNTRY is "WRONG" in AN OPPRESSIVE COUNTRY.

When we consider WHAT WE HAVE BECOME, maybe JESUS won't WANT TO RETURN.

If JESUS returned to OUR CURRENT WORLD, do you think HE WOULD WANT TO BE A CHRISTIAN?

A GOOD FRIEND is not only someone WE CAN AMICABLY TALK TO; it is someone WE CAN AMICABLY BE SILENT AROUND.

When some people ask us for advice, THEY WANT EASY ANSWERS to HARD QUESTIONS.

If WE DO NOT CONSTANTLY TALK TO SOME PEOPLE, they tend to believe "SOMETHING IS WRONG."

It is HARD TO BE HONEST ABOUT HISTORY, without some "REVISIONS," because HONEST HISTORY is VILE, OBNOXIOUS, CRUEL and INCREDIBLE.

In THIS UNCERTAIN and FALLIBLE LIFE, if you make someone A SAINT, they will do something SINFUL, and if you make someone a DEVIL, they will do something GOOD or NOBLE. Is that WHY SAINTS HAVE TO BE DEAD?

POLICE in AMERICA do A LOT OF GOOD THINGS, and a lot of Bad Things.

Sometimes, BLACK PEOPLE cannot DO "A BAD THING," without THE BAD THING being BLAMED ON THEIR BLACKNESS.

We cannot LOVE "THINGS," because WE CAN ONLY LOVE SENTIENT BEINGS, or BEINGS WHO CAN RETURN OUR LOVE.

We MEASURE too many people by their MONEY and MAKEUP.

Some people do not APPRECIATE OUR JOKES, because they are not THEIR JOKES.

We DO GOOD and BAD things in RAISING OUR CHILDREN, but WE WILL ONLY ACCEPT RESPONSIBILITY FOR THE GOOD.

LIFE cannot ALWAYS BE what we WANT IT TO BE, but IT CAN ALWAYS BE what WE MAKE IT.

Why would GOD GIVE US SOMETHING we have CHOSEN TO ONLY PRAY FOR, rather THAN WORK FOR?

INFANTS and TODDLERS are SO FRAGILE that WE OFTEN HARM THEM "UNWITTINGLY."

GOD is GENERALLY credited for GOOD THINGS; but THE LAW is the only entity BRAVE ENOUGH to BLAME GOD for some HORRIBLE or TERRIBLE THINGS or SOME CATASTROPHES.

MOST OF US can only "SEE" with OUR EYES.

We CANNOT ALWAYS HELP or SAVE PEOPLE just because WE WANT TO.

We cannot LIVE OUR LIVES WELL without TRUSTING SOME STRANGERS.

We do not always FEEL WHAT WE THINK, and WE DO NOT ALWAYS THINK ABOUT WHAT WE FEEL.

It is MOSTLY LIARS who are MOST AGGRESSIVE in DECLARING that THEY ARE TELLING THE TRUTH.

Do you THINK HIGH TECH DEVICES are making our lives EASIER or MORE COMPLICATED?

Were it not for OUR SYSTEM OF GOVERNANCE, some POLITICIANS would have NO QUALMS about ESTABLISHING A DICTATORSHIP in AMERICA.

WHY do we LITERALLY BELIEVE, that just because someone got A JOB in MOVIES or ON TELEVISION, that SOMEHOW makes THEM BETTER than THE REST OF US.

We cannot MAKE someone MATURE or SUCCESSFUL by GIVING THEM GOOD ADVICE.

We tend to believe WE DESERVE things WE CANNOT AFFORD.

WHAT is STRONGER in YOU, LOVE or LUST?

WE ARE probably The MOST DANGEROUS PERSON in OUR LIFE.

We can TELL what MOST PEOPLE THINK or FEEL by THEIR ATTITUDE.

Life is not only WHAT WE MAKE IT, but WHAT IT HAS MADE US.

It is not ALWAYS OTHER PEOPLE'S FAULT, when WE BECOME ANNOYED WITH THEM.

We want TO HELP or SAVE SOME PEOPLE, more THAN SOME PEOPLE WANT TO HELP or SAVE THEMSELVES.

*RIGHT CAN BE WRONG*

Some MARRIAGES can only TOLERATE "THE BETTER" and ARE DESTROYED by "THE WORSE."

ALL ROMANTIC RELATIONSHIPS begin SO GOOD, that is why they end SO BADLY.

We tend to HAVE MORE FAMILY than FRIENDS.

People who have THE LEAST TO SAY tend TO WANT TO DO MOST OF THE TALKING.

Sometimes, HOW WE DO SOMETHING is more important than WHAT WE DO.

Do we BELIEVE IN too MANY THINGS that ARE NOT REAL or DO NOT EXIST?

ULTIMATELY, the only PEOPLE we CAN HELP or SAVE are OURSELVES.

IN LIEU of "LOVE," there is ONLY "LUST" PULLING US TOGETHER.

We cannot BLAME LOVE, because so many people APPROACH IT "BLINDLY."

What we think of SINS or CRIMES depends on WHO IS COMMITTING THEM.

We are not likely to MAKE "THE WORLD" A BETTER PLACE, but we can MAKE "OUR WORLD" a BETTER PLACE.

We do not believe OTHER PEOPLE CAN SOLVE OUR PROBLEMS, but WE BELIEVE WE CAN SOLVE OTHER PEOPLE'S PROBLEMS.

When some people ADVISE us ABOUT OUR PROBLEMS, they are TELLING US WHAT IS BEST FOR THEM.

When most PEOPLE TRY TO EXPLAIN THEIR PROBLEMS to us, they ONLY EXPLAIN THEIR HURT or PAIN.

Most television TALK SHOWS are TOO HARD on the quests THEY DISLIKE and TOO EASY on the people THEY LIKE.

We do not ALWAYS KNOW what WE DON'T WANT, until WE GET IT.

When WE LAUGH AT or HATE PEOPLE; we are saying AS MUCH ABOUT OURSELVES as we are about THE PEOPLE upon whom WE ARE CASTING ASPERSIONS.

Some food companies THINK THEY ARE "FOOLING US," WHEN THEY DON'T RAISE THE PRICE, BUT JUST REDUCE THE CONTENT.

Many YOUNG PEOPLE cannot SEE THEIR Faults or FLAWS, so THEY CANNOT ADDRESS THEM; some ELDERLY PEOPLE can SEE THEIR FAULTS or FLAWS, but it is TOO LATE TO ADDRESS THEM.

In arguments, WE DO NOT LISTEN to LEARN; we listen to OVERTURN.

Some people BELIEVE that there are NO DEFINITIVE DEFINITIONS FOR "LOVE" or "GOD," because TO DEFINE THEM IS TO LIMIT THEM.

Some people who keep reminding us that they are "GOD FEARING," want us FEAR THEM more than GOD.

Some of OUR CHILDREN are MORE THAN WE CAN HANDLE.

If we CANNOT BE OURSELVES, we cannot BE ANYONE ELSE.

The world cannot LIVE IN HARMONY, because EVERYONE WANTS THE WORLD TO ONLY BE THE WAY THEY WANT THE WORLD TO BE.

It is ONLY SAFE "TO BE SILLY," around PEOPLE WHO LOVE, LIKE or CARE ABOUT US.

HAPPY MARRIAGES are SO VALUABLE, because THEY ARE SO RARE.

The WORST PART OF BEING HUMAN is that WE ARE NOT "INFALLIBLE" or "IMMORTAL."

Society has SO MANY PROBLEMS, because WE cannot "FORCE PEOPLE" to be THE KIND OF PEOPLE they AUGHT TO BE.

TELLING THE TRUTH can be JUST AS DANGEROUS as TELLING LIES.

In some COUNTRIES, those with THE MOST RIGHTS tend to DO THE MOST WRONGS.

SO MUCH OF OUR FATES or DESTINIES depend ON "THE PARENTS" WE WERE "ASSIGNED TO."

THE GRASS is not necessarily "GREENER ON THE OTHER SIDE," WE ARE JUST SICK OF LOOKING AT OUR OWN GRASS.

BEWARE OF all transactions INVOLVING MONEY; because then, THE GOLDEN RULE IS REVERSED: We want TO RECEIVE MORE THAN WE GIVE

*RIGHT CAN BE WRONG*

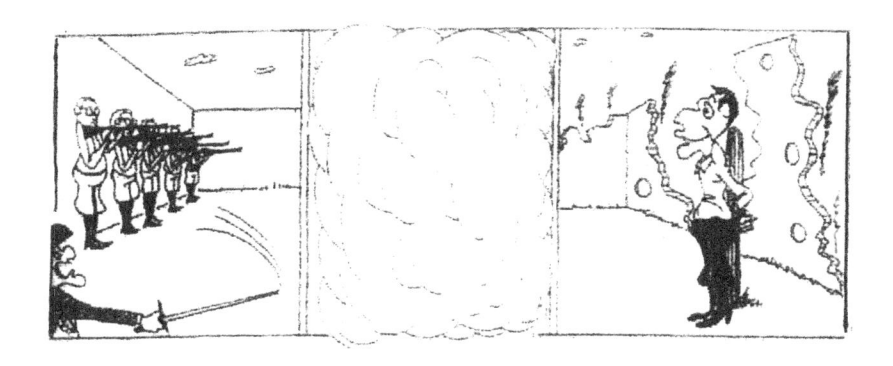

HOW we treat our children NOW is how THEY will treat us LATER.

MANY "gods" once WAS RIGHT, but now IT'S WRONG.

We cannot MOSTLY CHANGE THE WORLD; the world MOSTLY CHANGES US.

We ACCUSE OTHERS OF "HAVING ISSUES," as if WE DON'T.

CIVILIZATION is almost never TOTALLY AT PEACE; SOMEONE is ALWAYS FIGHTING SOMEONE. The GOAL of HUMAN-ANIMALS is still TO BECOME MORE HUMAN and LESS of AN ANIMAL.

Are more BAD THINGS HAPPENING, or are MORE BAD THINGS being VISUALLY RECORDED?

Why is it CONSIDERED "A SPORT" when TWO PEOPLE climb into A RING and TRY TO HURT or DESTROY EACH OTHER?

Have you EVER heard A RELIGIOUS LEADER ADMIT, that THEY DIDN'T KNOW SOMETHING about GOD or RELIGION? NO, because IF THEY DON'T KNOW SOMETHING, THEY MAKE SOMETHING UP.

It is GOOD that we cannot "KNOW EVERYTHING," because WE ALWAYS NEED SOMETHING NEW TO LEARN.

Though we HATE TO ADMIT IT, sometimes the people WE DISLIKE are RIGHT.

Do MEGA CHURCHES believe BIGGER is BETTER, because THE BIGGER THEY BUILD, the BETTER THEIR MONEY?

Most RELIGIONISTS are RELIGIOUS ONLY IN WORDS or RHETORIC.

Most of us CAN CONVINCE OURSELVES that GOD WANTS US TO DO ANYTHING WE WANT TO DO.

One of THE BEST THINGS about PET ANIMALS is that THEY STILL LOVE US after WE HAVE TREATED THEM BADLY.

One of THE FIRST LESSONS LIFE TEACHES OUR YOUNG, is that THEY ARE NOT AS SMART as THEY HAVE ALWAYS THOUGHT.

We are willing TO MITIGATE OUR MORALS, and RESTRAIN OUR CONDEMNATION, for PEOPLE WE LIKE.

The "MOST DANGEROUS PERSON" is A WEAK PERSON with STRONG POLITICAL POWER.

If there WERE "A SECRET" to LOVE, PEACE or HAPPINESS, someone would have REVEALED IT BY NOW.

If some people WHO WORRY A LOT, have nothing TO WORRY ABOUT, it WORRIES THEM.

We cannot always "DO THE RIGHT THING," because we cannot always DECIDE WHAT IS THE RIGHT THING TO DO.

WE ENJOY believing in GOD and LOVE, because THEY CAN BE whatever WE WANT THEM TO BE.

Can you THINK of ANYTHING that WE HUMANS WILL NOT DO FOR MONEY?

It is VERY DIFFICULT not to let GREAT SUCCESS "SWELL OUR HEADS."

There are OLD ELDERLY PEOPLE, and there are YOUNG ELDERLY PEOPLE.

Everyone is ALONE, that is why WE SO NEED ONE ANOTHER.

Do you ever WONDER how many GIFTED, TALENTED, or SPECIAL PEOPLE "THE LIMELIGHT" or "THE SPOTLIGHT" MISSES?

GENITALIA is all SOME ROMANTICS require of THEIR MATES.

We can NEVER find A MATE WITH "NO ISSUES;" we need to find a mate WHOSE ISSUES WE CAN TOLERATE.

Some people who ARE MARRIED, could never LIVE TOGETHER "IN SIN," and some people LIVING "IN SIN," could never last IN MARRIAGE.

EVERYONE thinks or believes THEY ARE "A GOOD PERSON," especially THE PEOPLE WHO ARE NOT.

Have you ever MET any of THOSE PEOPLE who CAME TO AMERICA WITH NOTHING, and NOW ARE BILLIONAIRES?

Many people think that they are IMPRESSING US when they ONLY SPEAK about GOD and SCRIPTURE.

Somewhere OUT THERE IN THE WORLD is A BLACK PERSON who does not believe THAT ALL WHITE CRITICISM of BLACK PEOPLE is RACIST. BUT NO ONE HAS EVER BEEN ABLE TO FIND THEM.

SOME MINISTERS, PREACHERS or RELIGIOUS LEADERS are GIVING US THEIR "PERSONAL OPINIONS" as to WHO or WHAT GOD and LOVE ARE.

How do WE KNOW THAT "EVERYTHING HAPPENS FOR A REASON," especially if WE DON'T KNOW THE REASON?

*RIGHT CAN BE WRONG*

Some BLACKS are "CULTURALLY WHITE," and SOME WHITES are "CULTURALLY BLACK."

We ENJOY LAUGHING AT EVERYTHING or EVERYONE except OURSELVES.

Everyone THINKS OF THEMSELVES as A GREAT PARENT, and THE WORST THING parents want to hear is THAT THEY ARE NOT A GREAT PARENT. THE PARENTS who are MOST OFFENDED are THE PARENTS WHO ARE NOT GREAT.

We do not "KNOW" some of the people WE FORM ROMANTIC RELATIONSHIPS WITH, because OUR ROMANTIC RELATIONSHIPS are mostly based on LIKE, LOOKS, LOOT, LUST and LUCK.

CELEBRITIES do not ALWAYS KNOW ONE ANOTHER; they deal with ONE ANOTHER based on REPUTATIONS, MONEY and RATINGS.

Many CON ARTISTS, CHARLATANS, SCAMMERS and FALSE PROPHETS hide under THE CLOAK of GOD or RELIGION.

GOD is A NON-DEFINITIVE, NON-DENOMINATIONAL, UNSEEN, UNIMAGINABLE, INDESCRIBABLE, LOVING, POSITIVE, MYSTERIOUS, OMNISCIENT, OMNIPOTENT and A PRESCIENT "SOMETHING," that we feel COMPELLED TO BELIEVE IN. Never has SOMETHING so UNKNOWN been SO FERVENTLY WORSHIPED.

If we SPEAK A TRUTH whose TIME HAS NOT COME, we may be SEVERELY PUNISHED.

Sometimes WE DON'T WANT TO HEAR THE TRUTH, because we are TOO LAZY to ACT ON IT.

TIME moves TOO SLOWLY FOR THE YOUNG and TOO QUICKLY FOR THE ELDERLY.

NATURE IS AMORAL; the ONLY ONES WHO CARES WHO WE HAVE SEX WITH, ARE PEOPLE.

SOME ARTS call themselves A SCIENCE, to increase THEIR CREDIBILITY.

Those people WHO DEFINE HAPPINESS, as being RICH and FAMOUS, need only to LOOK CLOSELY to see THAT VERY FEW RICH and FAMOUS PEOPLE seem GENUINELY HAPPY; they mostly JUST PRETEND TO BE. NOR are they necessarily BRILLIANT, SAINTLY or HEALTHY.

CHILDREN are always "A MIRACLE," but NOT ALWAYS "A BLESSING."

Some of us CANNOT BECOME INTELLECTUALS, because WE ARE TOO EMOTIONAL, and SOME OF US CANNOT BECOME EMOTIONALLY SENSITIVE, because we are TOO INTELLECTUAL.

Even RELIGIOUS PEOPLE are not "DYING TO GET TO HEAVEN."

OUR CHILDREN will ALWAYS SUFFER from some of OUR FAULTS and FLAWS.

RELIGIOUS PEOPLE "MOSTLY PREACH" and SAINTS "MOSTLY PRACTICE."

We have TROUBLE or DIFFICULTY DIFFERENTIATING LIKE, LUST and LOVE.

NOT ALL RELIGIOUS LEADERS are "TRUE BELIEVERS;" some are ONLY IN IT FOR THE MONEY, POWER and INFLUENCE.

We do not KNOW THE PEOPLE NEXT DOOR, but THINK WE KNOW CELEBRITIES AROUND THE WORLD.

A FEW PEOPLE ARE ABOVE THE LAW; THE POPE could probably GET AWAY WITH MURDER.

POP CULTURE is in the business of "PUSHING THE ENVELOPE."

No one CAN SEE THE FUTURE, but people cannot stop TELLING US, "WHAT'S BOUND TO HAPPEN."

We are HUMAN-ANIMALS, if we cannot solve problems HUMANELY, WE DECIDE TO FIGHT.

Some people who think that moving to a new location will solve their problems, ARE TRYING TO RUN AWAY FROM THEMSELVES.

LIFE and THE WORLD will ALWAYS NEED TO BE "HELPED" or "SAVED," because we can never ESCAPE OUR FALLIBILITY.

We are always in "THE RIVER OF LIFE," trying to FLOAT or SWIM, and hoping NOT TO DROWN.

BAD NEWS RUNS; GOOD NEW CRAWLS.

OPPRESSED PEOPLES want MORE FREEDOM, and so do FREE PEOPLE.

OUR LEADERS do not ALWAYS know WHAT'S BEST FOR US.

GOD WILL NOT HELP US, unless WE HELP GOD HELP US.

Some of OUR LEADERS are NOT AS SMART or AS MORAL as US.

*RIGHT CAN BE WRONG*

Do you think THAT MOST PEOPLE enter POLITICS, mostly for THE MONEY, THE GLORY, THE POWER or TO "SERVE THE PEOPLE."

Do WE ever BELIEVE THAT POOR PEOPLE CAN DO ANYTHING FOR THEMSELVES?

In AMERICA nearly EVERYTHING is DEFINED in MONEY TERMS or IN TERMS of BLACK and WHITE.

We want so much TO LIVE, that there is NO WAY to PREPARE FOR DEATH.

The only "ABSOLUTE GUARANTEE" in LIFE, is DEATH.

Some of THE GOOD THINGS we say about THE RECENTLY DEPARTED, are LIES.

The ONLY THING that "PHYSICAL ATTRACTIVENESS" can do IS "ATTRACT" – IT CANNOT "RETAIN."

MESSAGE TO YOUNG ROMANTICS: The most ATTRACTIVE PEOPLE among us are OFTEN CON ARTISTS, GOLD DIGGERS, SCAMMERS, CHARLATANS and EARTHLY DEVILS.

On EARTH, "DEVILS" always LOOK LIKE ANGELS.

TRUE or GENUINE LOVE never ENDS.

We have to say if LOVE is TRUE or GENUINE, because there are so many LOVE "IMPOSTORS."

ROMANTIC LOVE is mostly "CONDITIONAL."

We do not LIKE PEOPLE who are BETTER or WORST than us; we like people WHO ARE JUST AS GOOD or JUST AS BAD AS US.

Some of us CRAVE THE PRAISE of SOME PEOPLE, as much as WE CRAVE THE PRAISE of GOD.

Almost EVERYONE LIVES, as if they WILL NEVER DIE.

It is THE MISSION of SOME LAWYERS, to prove THAT A LIE is THE TRUTH, or THE TRUTH is A LIE.

All SERMONS either seek to appeal TO OUR MINDS, or TO OUR EMOTIONS.

There is NO ONE who DOESN'T CARE what ANYONE THINKS ABOUT THEM.

HOLLYWOOD almost NEVER THINKS that HISTORY is INTERESTING ENOUGH to be "PLAYED STRAIGHT."

SCIENTISTS, GENIUSES, SAINTS, SAGES or DEEP THINKERS are almost NEVER RICH or FAMOUS.

We PUNISH SOME CHILDREN for "BEING CHILDISH."

Do you ever WONDER if the people WHO SAY, "THEY ARE GOING TO PRAY FOR US" ever DO?

Don't TRY to "FIND" THE RIGHT PERSON, try TO "BE" THE RIGHT PERSON.

As HORRIFIC as WAR ALWAYS IS, how can any WAR BE "HOLY?"

We need TO STOP giving DEVILISH ACTIVITIES, GODLY NAMES.

If we JUGGLE TOO MUCH, we may NOT CATCH ANYTHING.

We are MORE HONEST in PRIVATE than IN PUBLIC.

When we MAKE A MISTAKE, we always want to EXPLAIN, in hopes that THE WHY will MITIGATE THE WHAT.

Things are ALWAYS CHANGING because WE have this tendency to ALWAYS BE DYING and BEING BORN.

OUR MISSION or CHALLENGE: How do we show OUR CHILDREN LIFE'S BEAUTY, and yet PROTECT THEM from ITS UGLINESS.

Is it REASONABLE TO ASSUME that ALL THINGS POSITIVE, LOVING, INSTRUCTIVE and that ENLARGES THE HUMAN SPIRIT is "GOD?"

Isn't it REASONABLE to SEE every book that is LOVING, POSITIVE, or INSTRUCTIVE, as important AS HOLY BOOKS; is not GOD within THESE BOOKS TOO? GOD is TOO HUGE to be RELEGATED TO JUST ONE BOOK.

In WAR, some of those "ON THE RIGHT SIDE," have also DONE SOMETHING "WRONG."

Can SOME THINGS be GOOD or GODLY, without directly MENTIONING GOODNESS or GOD?

If we seek A LIFE OF SECURITY, we must be willing to sacrifice some freedoms; but if we seek A LIFE OF FREEDOM, we must expect to experience SOME INSECURITY.

Do we SO ENJOY HEARING BAD NEWS ABOUT OTHERS, because we feel SO SMALL WITHIN OURSELVES that WE NEED TO FEEL SUPERIOR TO OTHERS?

No one REMEMBERS what LONG-WINDED SPEAKERS SAY.

LONG WINDED- SPEAKERS would rather LISTEN TO THEMSELVES, than SPEAK TO US.

*RIGHT CAN BE WRONG*

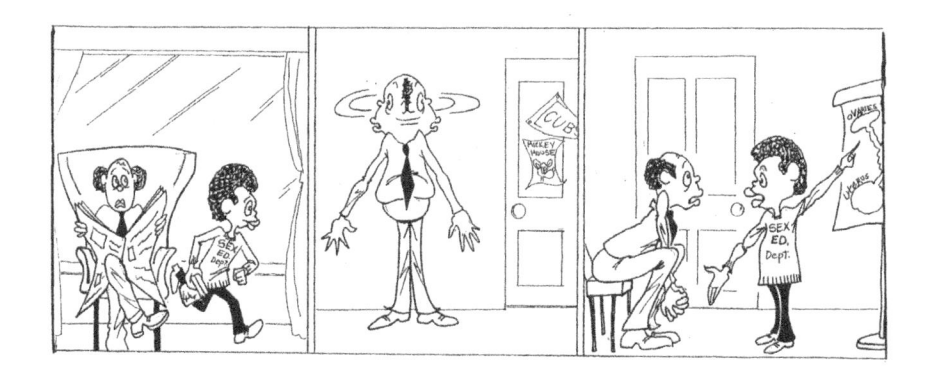

Do you think anyone Can BE ROLE MODELS for OUR YOUNG who is NOT RICH and/or FAMOUS?

What do RICH and FAMOUS people have that the rest of us don't have, OTHER THAN MONEY and NOTORIETY?

Some people look HEALTHY when they are OVERWEIGHT, and SICKLY when they LOSE WEIGHT.

MANY, if not MOST WOMEN assess ONE ANOTHER by PHYSICAL APPEARANCE; but MEN assess one another BY MONEY.

Can we DO NOTHING without RELIGION, or can RELIGION do nothing without US?

EVERYONE and EVERYTHING wants TO BE viewed as THE BIGGEST, THE BEST or THE BRIGHTEST.

EVERYTHING that is GREAT or that has MEANING, does not always HAVE ECONOMIC VALUE.

Most of US cannot "SEE" our OWN "BLINDNESS."

Are THE MIRACLES in HOLY BOOKS, MIRACLES or MAGIC?

PEOPLE in THE HOLY BOOKS would think PHONES, CARS, PLANES, COMPUTERS and TELEVISIONS were MIRACLES TOO.

Some celebrities DO NOT think THEY ARE DOING WHAT THEY LOVE, unless A LOT OF PEOPLE LOVE WHAT THEY DO.

In WAR, EVERYONE claims TO BE RIGHT, and EVERYONE can BE PROVEN TO HAVE COMMITTED SOME WRONGS.

Whatever is RIGHT TODAY, can be WRONG TOMORROW.

EVERYONE is RIGHT and WRONG.

NEVER TRY to name THE GREATEST, THE BIGGEST, THE BEST or THE BRIGHTEST, because you will always FORGET TO MENTION SOMEONE.

BLACK HISTORY is AMERICA'S "ILLEGITIMATE CHILD," for which IT IS ASHAMED.

The MORE people WE NEED TO LIKE US, the LESS WE TEND TO LIKE OURSELVES.

We do not BELIEVE we can LEARN ANYTHING from PEOPLE we DON'T LIKE.

For many, BEING MARRIED is TOUGH, and BEING SINGLE is TOUGH.

It is TOO EASY to call people "CRAZY" just because we do not LIKE THEIR BEHAVIOR.

The STRONGER WE ARE, the GENTLER WE MUST BE.

Because of our ACQUIRED ARROGANCE, nearly EVERYONE in AMERICA believes THAT WHEN they BECOME RICH and FAMOUS, it "QUALIFIES THEM" to GIVE ADVICE to ANYONE, regarding ANY SUBJECT.

THOSE who know HOW TO PREACH, do not tend TO PRACTICE, and those WHO KNOW HOW to PRACTICE, have NO NEED to PREACH.

To obtain MAXIMUM PHYSICAL HEALTH, we must learn TO STAY ACTIVE, and to obtain MAXIMUM SPIRITUAL HEALTH, we must learn TO BE STILL.

Most RELIGIOUS LEADERS and POLITICIANS don't NEED TO DO ANYTHING, except SAY SOMETHING TO INSPIRE US or MAKE US FEEL GOOD.

ALAS, Some of THE PEOPLE who most APPRECIATE AMERICA, are NOT AMERICANS.

We cannot tell others, THINGS THEY CANNOT UNDERSTAND.

CONTRARY to POPULAR BELIEF, many ELDERLY PEOPLE, do not FEAR DEATH.

It is MOSTLY YOUNG PEOPLE who FEAR DEATH or GETTING OLDER.

AGE seems TO SNEAK UP ON US, because WE DON'T NOTICE or PAY ATTENTION, until we are "OF A CERTAIN AGE."

Most of us WANT TO BE "THE BOSS," but we do not want to "PAY the COSTS."

Does it not BEHOOVE US to TRY TO "GROW" BEYOND our LUST or LIBIDO?

Never FALL IN LOVE with TELEVISION SHOWS, they will ALL EVENTUALLY LEAVE YOU.

We can have GREAT LOVE for OUR CHILDREN, without LIKING THEIR JOURNEY.

We do not ALWAYS AGREE WITH or UNDERSTAND THOSE who are NOT AS SMART AS US, and THOSE who are MUCH SMARTER THAN US.

Do all CHRISTIANS have to be "BORN-AGAIN," or are some READY- MADE?

When WE COMMIT A SIN or A CRIME, the best thing we can do is EXPRESS GREAT REMORSE; because NEXT TO CONDEMNING SIN and CRIME, what people MOST ENJOY Is FORGIVING THEM.

SINS OF THE FLESH are manifestations of PHYSICAL or PERSONAL WEAKNESS; but SINS OF THE SPIRIT are more likely to be AN EVIL ACT AGAINST OTHERS.

We CRAVE GOD, LOVE, PEACE and HAPPINESS so intensely, that IF WE CANNOT FIND THEM, we will "INVENT THEM."

A MIND without A HEART is A MAD or INSANE PERSON; A HEART without A MIND, is "A FOOLISH LOVER."

We do not mind ADMITTING that someone CAN RUN FASTER THAN US, or THAT SOMEONE IS A BETTER DANCER THAN US, but we HATE TO ADMIT that someone IS SMARTER THAN US.

ALL the CONCEPTS OF GOD are LARGE ENOUGH to include ALL RELIGIONS, but ALL RELIGIONS are not LARGE ENOUGH to include ALL OF THE CONCEPTS of GOD.

When LOGIC and REASON do not FIT our RELIGIOUS BELIEFS, we say, "GOD TRANSCENDS LOGIC and REASON"; but when LOGIC and REASON are CONSISTENT with OUR RELIGIOUS BELIEFS, we say, "IT ONLY MAKES SENSE."

Only MATURE PEOPLE can GENUINELY LOVE; whatever IMMATURE PEOPLE call LOVE, is "SOMETHING ELSE."

When PEOPLE WE DO NOT LIKE commit A SIN or CRIME, we CONDEMN THEM; but when SOMEONE WE LIKE, does the same, WELL, "WHO ARE WE TO JUDGE?"

Instead of CHANGING WHAT WE BELIEVE, to accommodate ALL THE NEW THINGS WE LEARN, we try TO CHANGE ALL THE NEW THINGS WE LEARN to accommodate WHAT WE ALREADY BELIEVE.

The "ONE-DROP RULE" was SO INSIDIOUS, because IT SAYS that ANY DROP of BLACK BLOOD, forever CONTAMINATES its HOST.

Most things WILL NOT turn out EXACTLY as WE WISH; they will TURN OUR BETTER or WORST.

When SOME RELIGIOUS PEOPLE announce THEY ARE "SAVED" --- SAVED FROM WHAT?

Are RELIGIOUS PEOPLE being "SAVED" from HELL? That would mean that THEY COULD DO NO WRONG.

The very "BEST PAY" for doing ANYTHING IN LIFE, is "GREATER SPIRITUAL JOY."

NO ONE should EVER be able to TELL US what WE CAN SEE, SPEAK, THINK, FEEL, BELIEVE, READ or LISTEN TO, if it does not involve direct injury to CHILDREN or ANIMALS.

Some FEMALES mostly want to have A RELATIONSHIP, and SOME MALES mostly want TO HAVE RELATIONS.

We know that FREEDOM and SECURITY are MUTUALLY EXCLUSIVE, but we still WANT TO HAVE IT BOTH WAYS.

In THE ABSENCE of CREDITABLE EVIDENCE, people WILL BELIEVE whatever THEY NEED TO BELIEVE; in THE PRESENCE of CREDITABLE EVIDENCE, people WILL BELIEVE whatever THEY NEED TO BELIEVE.

It is UNFAIR for us to say that life IS UNFAIR, because we are only concerned that LIFE IS UNFAIR TO US. We do not CARE that LIFE IS UNFAIR TO OTHERS. And that IS PRECISELY WHY LIFE IS SO UNFAIR.

We enjoy uttering VACUOUS STATEMENTS that SOUND GOOD, but are never GOOD AND SOUND: "WE NEED TO ALL COME TOGETHER" –ON WHAT BASIS? "WE NEED TO ALL TURN TO GOD" --- WHOSE GOD? "THE WORLD NEEDS TO CHANGE" – TO WHAT? "WHAT THE WORLD NEEDS IS MORE LOVE" –DEFINE LOVE? "WE NEED TO MAKE THIS A BETTER WORLD" -- DEFINE BETTER? "WE NEED TO STOP BEING SO SELFISH"— YOU STOP FIRST.

EVERYONE is "SELFISH"; it is EXTREMELY DIFFICULT for us to STOP BEING "SELFISH." The only time that SELFISHNESS is "A BAD THING," is when we MALICIOUSLY "USE OTHER PEOPLE" to ADVANCE OURSELVES, or WHEN WE REFUSE to AIDE or ASSIST the "HELPLESS."

THE LOWER THE PRICE, THE HIGHER THE RISK.

The FIRST THING young children LEARN is THE POWER and IMPORTANCE of "MONEY."

We do not just want A MATE who BELIEVES US – we want A MATE who WANTS TO BELIEVE US.

MONEY can ONLY HELP or ASSIST us PHYSICALLY; it CANNOT HELP or ASSIST us SPIRITUALLY.

POOR PEOPLE need MORE THAN MONEY; RICH PEOPLE need MORE THAN MONEY.

POVERTY is one of THE MOST EXPENSIVE THINGS in AMERICA.

WE ALWAYS THINK MONEY CAN DO MORE THAN MONEY CAN DO.

SEX is THE MOST PUBLICIZED, "PRIVATE THING" that HUMAN BEINGS DO.

It is sometimes THE SMALL THINGS that cause THE LARGE DISPUTES.

MARRIAGE is good for RAISING CHILDREN and A FEW ADULTS

Many WOMEN feel that RAISING CHILDREN is A BLESSING; many MEN feel that it is AN EXPENSE.

When WE FAIL, it was not ALL OUR FAULT, but WHEN WE SUCCEED, we did it ALL BY OURSELVES.

When people say, "THEY WANT TO CHANGE THE WORLD," we assume they mean FOR THE BETTER; and when people say, "THEY WANT TO PURSUE THEIR PASSIONS," we assume they mean THEIR POSITIVE PASSIONS.

Our OVERWHELMING IMPULSES causes us to CRAVE MONEY, FOOD, SEX, to be SELFISH, to desire POWER and SELF GLORIFICATION.

Just because WE CANNOT SEE "IT", doesn't necessarily mean THAT "IT" IS NOT THERE.

AMERICAN SLAVERY was ALL WRONG, because MOST PEOPLE thought that IT WAS ALL RIGHT. What we think IS "RIGHT CAN BE WRONG."

## RIGHT CAN BE WRONG

We OWN some things, and SOME THINGS OWN US.

In AMERICA, anyone or anything THAT LEGALLY EARNS A LOT OF MONEY is SOCIALLY ACCEPTABLE.

Some of us are MORE WILLING to LISTEN to A CELEBRITY than AN EXPERT.

Is it BETTER to earn A LOT OF MONEY, or BETTER to DO A LOT with LITTLE MONEY?

SEX is NOT THE MOST INTIMATE thing THAT TWO PEOPLE can SHARE; The MOST INTIMATE THING THAT TWO PEOPLE CAN SHARE, are SIMILAR SPIRITS or SIMILAR INTERESTS.

WOMEN mostly SUSTAIN "ORGANIZED RELIGION," but MEN are USUALLY "IN CHARGE."

Some people believe IT IS IMPORTANT TO BE NICE, and some people believe IT IS NICER TO BE IMPORTANT.

MANY women RESENT being seen AS ONLY SEX OBJECTS; SOME MEN TAKE PRIDE IN IT.

We cannot ADMIT WRONGS or MISTAKES; we try to JUSTIFY or RATIONALIZE WHATEVER WE DO.

Women who announce THAT "THEY DON'T NEED A MAN," are telling THEIR MALE CHILDREN that they are NOT NEEDED.

Our own INFIDELITY is SAD, but THE INFIDELITY of OTHERS is MOSTLY FUNNY.

The BEST THING we can FIND or DISCOVER is "OURSELVES."

EVERYONE in JAIL and HELL will CLAIM to be INNOCENT.

Those of us who do not feel VALUED will try to BUY IT.

Many of us LIE about OUR SEX LIVES and OUR MONEY.

POOR PEOPLE believe that their SALVATION lies in "OBTAINING MONEY," and RICH PEOPLE believe that their SALVATION lies in "GIVING MONEY AWAY."

SOME WOMEN believe that SEX is just "THE MEANS to AN END," and SOME MEN BELIEVE that SEX is "THE END by ANY MEANS."

WOMEN tend to be TOO NICE; MEN tend to be TOO NASTY.

STRONG MEN are seen as "PIT BULLS," but STRONG WOMEN are "BITCHES."

MEN have difficulty BECOMING FAITHFUL; WOMEN have difficulty REMAINING FAITHFUL.

Some WHITE PARENTS are seeing THAT INNER CITY INFLUENCE they fled the city to ESCAPE, in THE MUSIC of their SUBURBAN CHILDREN.

THE CHRISTIANITY, THE DAMAGE, THE HURT, THE MIXED BLOOD, and THE ENGLISH LANGUAGE are THE ONLY REMNANTS OF SLAVERY, that BLACK PEOPLE TODAY have not been ABLE TO "CAST OFF" with THEIR CHAINS.

BAD LAWS places GOOD PEOPLE in JAIL or PRISON.

MARRIED PEOPLE try to REMAKE ONE ANOTHER, into WHAT THEY want ONE ANOTHER TO BE.

We cannot GENUINELY LOVE OUR OWN, without LOVING "THE OTHERS"

BLACK PEOPLE are trying TO REMEMBER THEIR HISTORY, but WHITE PEOPLE are trying TO FORGET IT.

We cannot BE UP, without SOMEONE WANTING TO PULL US DOWN

The best way to find THE BEST MATE is to be OUR BEST SELF. We find THE BEST by BEING THE BEST.

The person WHO MARRIES MORE FOR LOOKS, will eventually LOOK FOR MORE.

FEAR GOES DOWN, the moment WE STAND UP.

A MOTHER is one WHO NURTURES a child, WHETHER BLOOD RELATED or NOT.

Our FALLIBLE LIVES are SO SCARY or INSECURE, that we feel COMPELLED to believe in A GREATER FORCE THAN OURSELVES; even if we do not FULLY UNDERSTAND what WE BELIEVE.

EVERYONE says of THE NEWLY DECEASED CELEBRITIES, "they will be missed." But The ONLY PEOPLE who will MISS THEM are their immediate FAMILY and FRIENDS.

When CELEBRITIES leave THE SPOTLIGHT, WE QUICKLY FORGET ABOUT THEM; that is WHY they try SO HARD and SO DESPERATELY to REMAIN THERE. NOTORIETY is WHAT THEY MOSTLY LIVE FOR.

Some are BLESSED to have had CHILDREN, and some are BLESSED, NOT to have HAD CHILDREN.

Some people do not believe ANYONE becomes WEALTHY, PLAYING solely BY THE RULES.

Some LAWS won't BE PASSED, until YOUNG PEOPLE grow up TO PASS THEM.

Money CAN NEVER "BUY HAPPINESS," but WE CAN NEVER STOP BELIEVING IT CAN.

RICH PEOPLE have BIG MONEY PROBLEMS or BIG MONEY UNHAPPINESS.

BULLIES are AFRAID of BULLIES who ARE BIGGER BULLIES THAN THEM.

Doctors RECEIVE CREDIT for MUCH of what OUR BODIES have NATURALLY DONE.

SOME BAD PARENTS "TODAY," are RAISING (or MIS-RAISING) "THE FUTURE PROBLEMS of TOMORROW."

When RICH PEOPLE reach the point WHERE THEY CAN AFFORD ANYTHING, people start GIVING THEM THINGS FOR FREE.

When A WHITE PERSON commits A CRIME, they are AN INDIVIDUAL; but WHEN A BLACK PERSON or MINORITY commits A CRIME, they are THEIR RACE or ETHNICITY.

The people who are MOST IMPRESSIVE are NOT TRYING TO IMPRESS ANYONE.

People with THE MOST CLASS do not feel the need TO ACT "CLASSY."

The QUICKEST WAY to start A RUMOR, is to tell people TO KEEP SOMETHING TO THEMSELVES.

If MANY AMERICANS lived SOUTH OF THE BORDER, they would be trying TO COME NORTH TOO.

## RIGHT CAN BE WRONG

TELEVISION knows that MOST OF ITS AUDIENCE will "EAT" whatever THEY ARE "FED".

ARGUMENTS and DEBATES are so CONTENTIOUS because NO ONE who HOLDS A STRONG OPINION ever THINKS THAT THEY ARE WRONG.

ADOLESCENTS LIE SO MUCH, because WORDS are THE ONLY "TOOLS" or "WEAPONS," they HAVE.

No one is ALWAYS RIGHT or CORRECT, especially THE EXPERTS.

JUSTICE in AMERICA is NOT ALWAYS PRETTY, because it is UNEVENLY APPLIED.

Some people think THEY ARE INFORMING US, when they tell us WHAT WE ALREADY KNOW.

The HELP that WE SEEK does not ALWAYS HELP.

Not ALL TEACHERS and POLICE OFFICERS deserve MORE PAY, only THE GOOD or GREAT ONES.

ADVERTISING or MARKETING doesn't just ASK PEOPLE TO BUY --- IT TELLS THEM WHAT TO BUY.

Our children are ALWAYS CHANGING, but we REMAIN ABOUT THE SAME.

When WOMEN RULE THE WORLD, they will BAN BOXING, BULLFIGHTING, THE SHOOTING of WILD ANIMALS and WAR.

Which do you think WE WORSHIP MOST: GOD or MONEY?

Do you ever FEEL as though EVERYONE is "CRAZY" or INSANE, except YOU?

We cannot GET MOST PEOPLE TO DO WHAT WE WANT THEM TO DO, but we can't STOP TRYING.

"THE TRUTH HURTS," that is why so many of us USE IT AS A WEAPON.

There are some people WE CANNOT GIVE ADVICE TO; we can only GIVE THEM A HUG.

PROSTITUTION should be LEGALIZED and TAXED to STOP "THE POLICE" from PROFITING FROM IT.

EVERYONE PROFITS from PROSTITUTION; The Prostitute, The "John," and The Police. EVERYONE except THE STATE and THE COUNTRY.

EVERYTHING ultimately MAKES SENSE, even THE NONSENSE.

Do not believe those people who WANT US TO BELIEVE that THEY "HAVE FUN" ALL THE TIME, because that would be AS BORING as WORKING ALL THE TIME.

Sometimes we know WHAT WE MEAN, we just can't find the words TO SAY IT.

We NEVER KNOW what HURT FEELINGS or WOUNDED PRIDE will do TO RETALIATE, GET EVEN or "SAVE FACE."

We keep WANTING, EXPECTING, and PUSHING PEOPLE to be BETTER than THEY ARE CAPABLE OF BEING.

Almost no children are AS GREAT as THEIR PARENTS BELIEVE or HOPE THEY ARE.

MANY OF US are not AS GREAT as WE THINK WE ARE.

Sometimes, WE HAVE TO BE CONTENT with WHO WE ARE NOW and WHAT WE ALREADY HAVE ATTAINED.

For some of us, SIN is EXCITING and SAINTLINESS is TOO POMPOUS or BORING.

Most of us WHO BELIEVE our way of THINKING or BELIEVING is BEST, have NEVER THOUGHT or BELIEVED in ANY OTHER WAY.

No one can "SAVE US" but US; but that doesn't stop ANYONE from thinking THEY CAN "SAVE" SOMEONE ELSE.

We do not always ACKNOWLEDGE "THE PRESENT," we are ALWAYS THINKING ABOUT "THE PAST" or "THE FUTURE."

Some of us POSSESS A RELIGION and some of us ARE POSSESSED by A RELIGION.

KNOWLEDGE can be EXPRESSED by WORDS, but LOVE is best EXPRESSED by ACTIONS.

Why do ELDERLY WOMEN refer to one another AS "GIRLS," and ADOLESCENT YOUNG MALES, refer to one another AS "MAN?"

All THE "STARS" try TO OUTSHINE ONE ANOTHER.

Most of us want to be BIGGER, BETTER and BRIGHTER than we will EVER BE.

WHAT WE THINK often includes WHAT WE BELIEVE or WHAT WE FEAR.

We can sometimes HELP or ASSIST ONE ANOTHER, in ways that we CAN'T HELP or ASSIST OURSELVES.

Some people are willing TO DIE to ENTER HEAVEN, and SOME ARE WILLING TO DIE TO ENTER AMERICA.

Elderly people FEEL SUPERIOR, because THEY HAVE LIVED LONG; YOUNG PEOPLE FEEL SUPERIOR because THEY ARE STILL YOUNG.

Is it FAIR for us TO COMPARE our "REAL LIFE" to "THE FAKE LIFE" of POP CULTURE?

Our CONCEPT or BELIEF in GOD or LOVE, will only be AS MATURE as WE ARE.

Most of us want the world TO BECOME A BETTER PLACE, but we want SOMEONE ELSE TO DO IT.

When people call MEAN PEOPLE MEAN, mean people are usually TOO MEAN to see their OWN MEANNESS.

We have been MOST DECEIVED if we never KNOW we have BEEN DECEIVED.

Some of us HAVE A JOB and some of OUR JOBS HAVE US.

There are ILLEGAL THIEVES and THERE ARE SOME "LEGAL THIEVES."

LIFE is rarely FAIR; it is mostly TOO BITTER or TOO SWEET.

THE POSITIVES do ALL THE GOOD WORKS, but THE NEGATIVES get all THE ATTENTION.

SMALL CHILDREN have NO IDEA what THEY WANT TO BE WHEN THEY GROW UP.

We cannot STOP THINKING of GOD as A PERSON.

If we could ESTABLISH how much MONEY WAS "ENOUGH," no one would think ENOUGH WAS ENOUGH.

There are TWO KINDS of POOR PEOPLE: Those WHO CAN'T HELP THEMSELVES, and THOSE WHO WON'T HELP THEMSELVES.

IN AMERICA, the CONDITIONS of THE POOR bother US ALL, more than THEY BOTHER THE POOR.

STRONG MEN know WHEN TO CRY and STRONG WOMEN know WHEN NOT TO.

TO PLAY THE GAME we must know HOW THE GAME IS PLAYED.

ULTIMATELY, everyone in a ROMANTIC RELATIONSHIP MUST ASK THEMSELVES what is it MOSTLY ABOUT: Is it about LOVE, is it about MONEY or is it about SEX?

There are TWO WAYS to look AT LIFE: The MASCULINE WAY and THE FEMININE WAY.

We do not KNOW what WE HAVE GOTTEN INTO, until WE HAVE GOTTEN INTO IT.

Some of us LOVE MARRIAGE more than WE LOVE OUR SPOUSE.

Some of the ways WE PUNISH OUR CHILDREN are AS WRONG or AS BAD AS THE CHILDREN.

CHILDREN REMEMBER what THEIR PARENTS FORGET.

Are ARRANGED MARRIAGES better or worse THAN THE MARRIAGES THAT WE CHOOSE for OURSELVES?

Do you think YOUR PARENTS could CHOOSE A BETTER MATE for you THAN YOU CAN CHOOSE for YOURSELF?

How do you think PACIFISTS would HAVE DEALT WITH HITLER?

Do PACIFISTS believe ANYTHING IS WORTH FIGHTING FOR?

It is INCREDIBLY DIFFICULT to be NICE to NASTY PEOPLE.

WOMEN live longer THAN MEN, because they have MORE "EXTRA-MEDICAL RELATIONSHIPS" with DOCTORS than MEN.

SOME of WHAT WE EXPECT is sometimes interrupted by SOMETHING WE DIDN'T EXPECT.

SOME RELIGIOUS LEADERS have DICTATORIAL POWERS.

ARROGANT PEOPLE, HOLY BOOKS and RELIGIONISTS have AN ANSWER FOR EVERYTHING.

ANY ENTITY that says IT HAS ALL THE ANSWERS should be viewed AS QUESTIONABLE.

PERHAPS we need MORE SAINTS IN POLITICS and MORE DEMOCRACY in RELIGION.

SMART or WISE PEOPLE rarely say DUMB or FOOLISH THINGS, HAPPY PEOPLE rarely BOAST or BRAG, STRONG PEOPLE rarely FLEX THEIR MUSCLES, and LOVING PEOPLE rarely say HATEFUL THINGS.

If we ACCEPT ACCOUNTABILITY for ANYTHING, we will probably BE BLAMED FOR SOMETHING.

Many POLITICIANS are TORN between GETTING MORE FOR THEMSELVES, being FAITHFUL TO THEIR IDEOLOGY, and SERVING THE COUNTRY.

How people "SEE US" is HOW THEY TREAT US.

How can RICH or FAMOUS PEOPLE tell WHEN PEOPLE sincerely CARE ABOUT THEM?

Why does IT SEEM that when we have A MINOR AILMENT or AUTO MALFUNCTION, they DISAPPEAR when WE TAKE THE PROBLEMS TO A PROFESSIONAL?

The WORST THING THE MAJORITY can do to any of THE MINORITY, is to treat them like A MINORITY.

If some CELEBRITIES knew about US, they would ENVY or ADMIRE US TOO.

A DEFINITION FOR "DISCIPLINE": The ABILITY to DO whatever WE DO NOT WANT TO DO, but AUGHT to DO, or THE ABILITY to STOP DOING whatever WE WANT TO DO and DO WHAT WE AUGHT TO DO.

We tend to BELIEVE our COUNTRY is THE GREATEST or THE BEST, because IT IS WHERE WE LIVE.

Some of us are MORE AFRAID OF LIFE than DEATH.

We cannot be ABSOLUTELY SURE that these are THE LAST DAYS for EVERYONE, but THEY ARE ALWAYS THE LAST DAYS for SOMEONE.

People have been PREDICTING THE END OF THE WORLD, since THE BEGINNING OF THE WORLD.

There is NOTHING that MORE "DIVIDES" THE HUMAN RACE than RACISM and ORGANIZED RELIGION, which PREACHES "UNIVERSAL LOVE."

Do you think that people WHO PREACH, should have TO PROVE WHAT THEY SAY? And RELIGIOUS PEOPLE should WORK HARDER for what THEY ONLY PRAY FOR.

Many SPIRITUAL LEADERS and PREACHERS in AMERICA are trying to OUT BUILD, OUT LEARN, OUT PREACH, OUT GROW and OUT SHINE ONE ANOTHER.

The WORLD is DESIGNED and STRUCTURED for THE YOUNG, but they are NEVER QUALIFIED to be IN CHARGE.

People will not GROW UP, just because we tell them to "GROW UP."

HOW WE SEE and WHO WE ARE is DETERMINED by what AGE WE ARE, and IN WHAT "AGE" WE LIVE IN.

Some people LIVE THEIR LIVES "FIXATED AT A CERTAIN AGE" or PERIOD OF TIME.

We cannot believe EVERYTHING PEOPLE SAY, but WE CAN BELIEVE MOST THINGS THEY DO.

LYING can sometimes BE LOVING, and THE TRUTH can sometimes BE CRUEL.

Some of us are not WHO WE SAY WE ARE, we are WHO WE WON'T SAY WE ARE.

Sometimes things that do not GLITTER can be GOLD.

We do not KNOW what WILL HAPPEN IN THE FUTURE; and we do not ALWAYS KNOW what happened in THE PAST.

Sometimes, we can SPEAK SUCH TRUTH, that we will be called LIARS, and we can be SO RIGHT, that EVERYONE will think WE ARE WRONG.

NO RICH PERSON is WILLING to FORFEIT THEIR FORTUNE for ANYONE or for ANYTHING. The only way we can GET THEIR MONEY, is when they die.

We CANNOT convince MOST PEOPLE that THEY CAN be HAPPY or SUCCESSFUL, WITHOUT HAVING A LOT OF MONEY.

It is SO DIFFICULT to MAKE A BETTER WORLD, because HOW BETTER IS DEFINED depends on WHICH PART OF THE WORLD WE ARE IN.

We cannot REACH CONSENSUS on WHAT CONSTITUTES "A BETTER WORLD"; this is, after all, WHAT WE FIGHT WARS ABOUT.

We cannot ALWAYS believe WHAT "THEY SAY."

Almost NO ONE asks themselves IF THEY WOULD BE A GOOD PARENT, we just ASSUME WE WOULD.

ALL PARENTS are TEACHERS and ALL TEACHERS are PARENTS.

IN THE PHYSICAL or MATERIAL WORLD, "LOOKS" are EVERYTHING; in "THE SPIRITUAL WORLD," they mean NOTHING.

We are not GOOD or GREAT PEOPLE, unless GOOD or GREAT PEOPLE THINK SO.

No matter HOW CONFIDENT people PRETEND TO BE, we are ALL "INSECURE," mainly BECAUSE WE ARE FALLIBLE and MORTAL.

SICKNESS and DEATH humbles US ALL.

The MORE WE TALK, the less PEOPLE LISTEN.

IN WARS, both sides TEND to COMMIT "CRIMES AGAINST HUMANITY." It is "THE WINNER" who DECIDES what is MOST HEINOUS or who is MOST CULPABLE.

We do not LOVE ALL TEACHERS, unless WE AGREE WITH WHAT THEY ARE TEACHING.

Almost EVERYONE WE TELL OUR PROBLEMS TO, WILL TRY TO SOLVE THEM FOR US.

If we tried to regularly KEEP IN TOUCH with all OUR ACQUAINTANCES, FRIENDS and FAMILY, we would spend TOO MUCH OF OUR TIME just KEEPING IN TOUCH.

We have CEASED mostly CELEBRATING "QUALITY" and "SUBSTANCE" and have begun mostly LAUDING CREDENTIALS, CELEBRITIES and BEST SELLERS.

SOMETIMES, LOVE cannot CONQUER HATE.

We want things TO BE SO RIGHT, that we sometimes FORGET that THINGS can GO WRONG.

Is there A SIGNIFICANT DIFFERENCE between PRAYER and WISHING and HOPING?

When we BECOME RICH, we tend to want to BECOME RICHER.

LIFE, or "THE UNIVERSE" does not care about OUR HOPES, WISHES or DREAMS.

It BEHOOVES US not to just LOVE OUR MATE, but to also ADMIRE THEM, if we can.

WHY didn't GOD STOP PRIESTS from HARMING SMALL CHILDREN?

In THE FUTURE, "WHITES" will become "THE LARGEST MINORITY."

Are there ANY WHITE PEOPLE who FEAR that one day BLACKS and MINORITIES will EVER DO TO THEM, what THEY HAVE DONE TO BLACKS and MINORITIES in AMERICA?

BLACK AMERICANS have SHOWN LOVE for AMERICA, at times WHEN AMERICA has not SHOWN LOVE FOR THEM.

If it is WRONG TO KILL PEOPLE, why isn't it WRONG TO KILL KILLERS? Who will be THE BIGGER PERSONS?

Must NEARLY EVERY POPULAR SONG be about SEX and/or ROMANCE?

TEEN-AGERS are DIFFICULT to DEAL WITH, because they are NEITHER CHILDREN nor ADULTS.

One way to become RICH, is to LIVE LIKE we are POOR.

Some BLACK people WISH THEY WERE WHITE, and some WHITE PEOPLE wish THEY WERE BLACK ATHLETES and ENTERTAINERS.

LET CELEBRITIES BE; if people were CONSTANTLY SCRUTINIZING every inch OF YOU, you would WANT A NEW FACE and BODY TOO.

"MISERY LOVES COMPANY," but "VICTORY" and "SUCCESS" prefer TO BE ALONE.

Do you believe LOVE is more OF THE MIND, or MORE OF THE HEART?

OVER TIME, we either MOSTLY HELP or MOSTLY HARM our CHILDREN.

We are always CHANGING, for BETTER or FOR WORSE.

We begin by TRYING TO CHANGE THE WORLD, then WE TRY TO CHANGE ONE ANOTHER, but WE END UP just TRYING TO CHANGE OURSELVES.

We keep WANTING TO CHANGE PEOPLE or FIX PEOPLE, because NO ONE IS TOTALLY SATISFIED with the way ANYONE IS, or THE WAY WE ourselves ARE.

In some communities, THE POLICE are MORE THE PROBLEM than THE SOLUTION.

The HARDEST and MOST DIFFICULT THING TO DO --- is NOTHING.

We are sometimes TOO GENERAL about SPECIFICS and TOO SPECIFIC about GENERALITIES.

Great ACTS OF LOVE do not REQUIRE RECIPROCATION.

We are not "SEEKERS OF TRUTH," unless WE ARE UPSETTING THOSE WHO LIE.

Because of OUR HISTORY, most AMERICAN'S THINKING is FIXATED into A BLACK/WHITE DICHOTOMY.

In AMERICA we do not REVERE THE ELDERLY, because we see them as being IN PROXIMITY to DEATH, which is WHAT WE MOST FEAR.

Most people do not want to TELL US WHAT WE WANT TO HEAR; most people want to tell us WHAT THEY WANT TO HEAR.

We are not DONE until we are DEAD, stop THE AGEISM: We cannot ALWAYS TRUST the AVERAGES and THE STATISTICS. Some of the elderly are not "OLD," some are "YOUNG."

The two GROUPS THAT ARE MOST MISUNDERSTOOD, are those WHO ARE FAR BEHIND, and THOSE WHO ARE FAR AHEAD.

If we THINK too far "OUTSIDE THE BOX," we will not BE ALLOWED to REMAIN INSIDE THE BOX.

There are TOO MANY "LITTLE PEOPLE" running FOR HIGH OFFICES.

People who ACCUSE US of THINKING WE ARE BETTER THAN THEM, are sometimes ONLY PEOPLE WHO THINK THEY ARE LESS THAN US.

INCESSANT TALKERS do not know that they don't need to "SAY" everything THEY THINK, FEEL or BELIEVE in a single conversation.

In AMERICA, THE WELFARE SYSTEM GIVES PEOPLE INCENTIVE NOT TO GET MARRIED.

Many people do not WANT TO ASSIST US IN BECOMING OURSELVES; they want to ASSIST US IN BECOMING THEM.

The BIGGEST LIE WE CAN TELL, is to tell people "WE NEVER LIE."

No one KNOWS A LOT ABOUT A LOT; we MUST SPECIALIZE.

One of THE MOST LOADED QUESTIONS, is to ask A MARRIED MAN if HE HAS CHEATED: If we SAYS NO, he will BE NOT BELIEVED; if HE SAYS YES, he will BE CONDEMNED.

MEN who are ACCUSED OF INFIDELITY are generally CONSIDERED to be GUILTY until PROVEN INNOCENT.

JUST AFTER SLAVERY, the only PROFESSIONS offered BLACK PEOPLE were TEACHING and PREACHING.

The TOUGHEST BOSS that we can ever have IS WHEN WE WANT TO BE OUR OWN BOSS.

EVERYONE expects and believes "GOD is ON THEIR SIDE," regardless of WHAT SIDE THEY ARE ON.

SINNERS tend to be TOO SELFISH and RELIGIOUS PEOPLE tend to be TOO SELF-RIGHTEOUS.

OUR CHILDREN cannot be OUR FRIENDS, until THEY BECOME SELF SUFFICIENT.

We are ALL trying to REACH SOME DESTINATION, but only A FEW OF US KNOW THE "BEST ROADS" TO TAKE.

Lots of things are LEGAL, that are ILLOGICAL or ILL-ADVISED. And some things are ILLEGAL, that are not harmful to society.

Some children SURVIVE their PROBLEMATIC PARENTS and SOME DO NOT.

Of all THE OPPRESSION that WHITE PEOPLE like to CITE FOR LEAVING ANY PLACE IN THE WORLD to come to AMERICA, none of it CONSISTED of BEING DEPRIVED of THEIR NAMES, THEIR FAMILIES, THEIR HISTORY or ALL THEIR HUMAN FREEDOMS. They did not come here IN CHAINS, and they were not treated AS LESS THAN ANIMALS.

The BETTER WAY to "GET EVEN" is TO BECOME A BETTER PERSON.

There is not ENOUGH NEWS to FILL THE 24/7 NEWS CYCLE, so we are "PUNISHED" by CONSTANT REPETITION.

We either MOSTLY UNDERSTAND HOLY BOOKS, or MOSTLY MISUNDERSTAND HOLY BOOKS.

Some MARRIAGES are A MISTAKE, and some DIVORCES are A MISTAKE.

The moment we say WHAT A PERSON IS or IS NOT CAPABLE OF BEING or DOING, someone will DEBUNK IT.

We cannot BE anything we WANT TO BE, we can only BE MORE OF WHAT WE ALREADY ARE.

HAPPY PEOPLE do not need a reason, BECAUSE THEIR HAPPINESS is WHO THEY ARE, NOT WHAT THEY HAVE ATTAINED.

We like RELIGIOUS PEOPLE who PRACTICE WHAT THEY PREACH, and SINNERS WHO CAN BREAK ALL THE RULES with IMPUNITY.

We do A LOT OF DUMB THINGS to PROVE HOW SMART WE ARE.

If we BELIEVE there are POSITIVE and NEGATIVE INFLUENCES and IMPULSES in LIFE, does it really matter whether we call them GOD and DEVIL, GOOD and BAD, or RIGHT and WRONG?

Whether "BLOOD IS THICKER THAN WATER," is not always CLEAR.

The kind of "JUSTICE" we receive does not ALWAYS DEPEND ON THE LAW, sometimes IT DEPENDS ON The TEMPERAMENT OF POLICE OFFICERS or THE JUDGES.

Is it FAIR, that MARRIED ACTORS can" MAKE OUT" with people they are NOT MARRIED TO but the rest of us MARRIED PEOPLE CANNOT?

Children sometimes DISAPPOINT US, because we expect them TO BE AS MATURE AS WE ARE.

Some POLITICIANS do not think WITH THEIR HEADS; they think WITH THEIR POLITICAL HOPES, WISHES and DREAMS.

People are ALWAYS CLAIMING THAT THINGS are REAL, that they ARE "KEEPING IT REAL." It is very difficult TO FIND THE REAL REAL.

The only way AMERICA can SOLVE HER VIOLENCE PROBLEM is with MORE SECURITY; but the more SECURITY it has, the LESS FREEDOM.

We tend to be TOO SMARMY or WARM to the people WE LIKE, and TOO COLD or CALLOUS to THE PEOPLE WE DISLIKE.

The BETTER WAY to DISLIKE SOMEONE is to do it WITHOUT THEM KNOWING IT.

No matter WHOM we DECIDE is THE BIGGEST, THE BEST, or THE BRIGHTEST, someone NEW will eventually COME FORTH who is EVEN BIGGER, BETTER or BRIGHTER.

Some CONGRESSIONAL COMMITTEES will CODDLE people THEY LIKE, and BULLY people THEY DISLIKE.

Most of our PROBLEMS, CRIMES and SINS, are CAUSED BY ILLICIT MONEY and SEX.

MONEY and SEX are BAD THINGS, except WHEN THEY ARE GOOD THINGS.

All some of us need TO SUCCEED in LIFE is GOOD LUCK.

HOW TO AVOID ARGUMENTS: People DON'T WANT TO HEAR WHAT THEY DON'T WANT TO HEAR.

Some of us ARE SLOWLY COMMITTING SUICIDE or KILLING OURSELVES over OUR LIFETIME.

We are all "PARTIALLY BLIND," because THERE IS ALWAYS SOMETHING WE CANNOT SEE.

Just because WE ARE LOOKING AT SOMETHING, does not necessarily MEAN THAT WE CAN SEE IT.

Our ability TO LEARN MORE must always be based ON WHAT WE ALREADY KNOW.

To ENLIGHTEN or EDUCATE OTHERS, means, TO LIGHTEN "THE DARKNESS" of PEOPLE or TO AWAKEN PEOPLE WHO ARE "SLEEPING."

Do not ENVY PEOPLE who HAVE MORE MONEY than you. ENVY THOSE who have DONE MORE WITH THEIR MONEY or WHO HAVE BEEN MORE CREATIVE.

The most IMPRESSIVE THING that GREAT WEALTH can BUY, is POWER and INFLUENCE.

TODAY, MEN mostly MEASURE or ASSESS THEMSELVES by MONEY and THEIR SEXUAL PROWESS, and WOMEN, by THEIR PHYSICAL APPEARANCE and THEIR FAMILIES.

There are LIMITS to WHAT MONEY CAN BUY, but no limits to HOW MUCH MONEY CAN BUY.

HAVING A LOT OF MONEY cannot GUARANTEE HAPPINESS but NOT HAVING ANY MONEY can INSURE SADNESS.

Most of us are not concerned with whether we ARE LOVING, we only care about if WE ARE LOVED.

MOST PEOPLE who are SMART, ATTRACTIVE, HEALTHY and RICH, have A FALSE SENSE of THEIR OWN INVINCIBILITY.

Do you THINK MOST PEOPLE speak INTELLIGENTLY or LOGICALLY or DO MOST PEOPLE speak EMOTIONALLY or SELFISHLY?

Some people CAN SAY MORE by SAYING LESS.

LIFE is "A JIGSAW PUZZLE" that EVERYONE MUST PUT TOGETHER, MOSTLY ALONE.

Sometimes, WE CANNOT THINK STRAIGHT, because of THINGS we are AFRAID TO THINK ABOUT.

THE IDEALISTS see LIFE as BEAUTIFUL. THE PESSIMISTS see LIFE as UGLY. THE REALISTS see LIFE as BOTH BEAUTIFUL and UGLY.

It is EXCEEDINGLY DIFFICULT to MAKE WAR, MAKE SENSE.

Do you wish WE WOULD STOP making people WHO WERE LUCKY ENOUGH to become RICH and/or FAMOUS, into MINOR GODS and GODDESSES?

Many people who tell us, "THEY CAN HANDLE THE TRUTH," are LYING. THE TRUTH is the most DIFFICULT THING in LIFE TO HANDLE; that is WHY WE LIE SO MUCH.

THE LIVES OF PEOPLE who PREDICT THE END OF THE WORLD, always END before THE WORLD DOES.

RICH PEOPLE hope THEIR CHILDREN will "HIGHLY APPRECIATE" the MONEY THEY LEAVE THEM, that THEY DID NOT WORK FOR.

After WE ARE GONE, some of OUR CHILDREN will TRASH some of our TREASURES.

Most PEOPLE are willing TO SHARE OUR JOY; but ONLY THOSE WHO LOVE US are WILLING TO SHARE our PAIN.

Trying to PLEASE EVERYONE, can MEAN PLEASING NO ONE.

We keep complaining about THE POLARITY in POLITICS. The FOUNDERS OF AMERICA anticipated such things, and placed CHECKS and BALANCES to GUARD AGAINST this CYCLE which is so prevalent in DEMOCRACY. AMERICA was DESIGNED to be A COUNTRY, where WE CAN ALL PEACEFULLY AGREE TO DISAGREE.

All GOOD ADVICE to people is mostly LOGICAL or REASONABLE; except that PEOPLE are not ALWAYS LOGICAL or REASONABLE.

JUSTICE in AMERICA is sometimes NEGOTIABLE.

People on THE RIGHTEOUS SIDE tend to be SANCTIMONIOUS in CONDEMNING those ON THE WRONG SIDE.

LOVE does not REQUIRE A RELIGION, but MOST RELIGIONS PREACH LOVE.

We are NOT HAPPY, unless we can HANDLE UNHAPPINESS WELL.

We cannot DO ANYTHING GOOD or GREAT, unless WE CAN GET PASS the RESISTING FORCES in LIFE, that DO NOT WANT US TO BECOME GOOD or GREAT.

We are BORN INTO LIFE, by CHANCE, LUCK, or HAPPENSTANCE: OUR PARENTS, OUR RACE or ETHNICITY, OUR PHYSICALITY, OUR SOCIAL or ECONOMIC CLASS, OUR GENDER, OUR RELATIVES and OUR RELIGION. And ALL OF IT MAKES TOO MUCH OF A DIFFERENCE FOR THE REST OF OUR LIVES.

It is difficult TO ADVISE ANYONE about ANYTHING, because MOST OF US will not LISTEN to ANYTHING that WE DO NOT WANT TO HEAR.

We tend to OVERLOOK THE OBVIOUS and IGNORE THE COMPLEX.

It can CONFUSE US when WE LOVE some people WE DO NOT LIKE, or LIKE some people WE COULD NEVER LOVE.

We tend TO BE in LOVE with LOVE.

OUR YOUNG will ask FOR OUR MONEY but NOT OUR ADVICE, because THEY CAN REPAY MONEY, but THEY WANT TO PROVE TO US THAT THEY DON'T NEED OUR ADVICE.

MESSAGE TO ROMANTICS: Try to SEE a PERSON'S SPIRIT, as well AS THEIR BEAUTIFUL or SEXY BODIES.

Some RELIGIOUS GROUPS cannot RESIST THE APPEAL of POP CULTURE --- SO THEY RELIGIOUSLY IMITATE IT.

The ONLY WAY some of us WANT TO ASSIST or HELP OTHERS, is to ASSIST or HELP OTHERS to be MORE LIKE US.

Has EVERYTHING necessarily FAILED, just because IT WON'T SELL?

In POP CULTURE, people are RATED or RANKED according to HOW MANY PEOPLE LIKE or LOVE THEM; in REAL LIFE, we are LOVING, according to HOW MANY PEOPLE WE CAN LOVE.

Most people ARE AFRAID to CHALLENGE or QUESTION what they have BEEN TAUGHT or TOLD, because IT UPSETS their VIEW of REALITY, and THEIR SENSE of THEIR PERSONAL IDENTITY.

We do not have to LIKE PEOPLE in order to treat them with LOVING KINDNESS.

Some WHITE PEOPLE believe THAT SOME BLACK PEOPLE use their SLAVERY PAST as "A CRUTCH." SOME BLACK PEOPLE use THEIR SLAVERY PAST as A CRUTCH, because THEY HAVE BEEN SEVERELY CRIPPLED.

If we sincerely WANTED TO KNOW WHAT OUR FAULTS and FLAWS WERE, we WOULD ASK SOME OF THE PEOPLE WHO DO NOT LIKE US.

The more AWARDS or ACCOLADES we receive, THE LESS EACH ONE MEANS.

Not ALL AWARDS are HONESTLY EARNED but are the results of "WHEELING AND DEALING" by "THE BOSSES."

We do not always realize how FUNNY we are, when we are being SERIOUS, or how SERIOUS some of OUR JOKES ARE.

Do not expect people who are trying TO GET YOUR MONEY to BE TOTALLY HONEST with you.

We cannot become A BETTER PERSON, unless we are prepared to HEAR THE WORST about ourselves.

Some MOVIES are NOT SUITABLE for ADULTS.

We find it hard TO DO what NO ONE ELSE is DOING.

We say THAT "FAMILY COMES FIRST," but we MOSTLY BELIEVE that "WE COME FIRST."

Many RELIGIOUS PEOPLE do not AGREE WITH EVERYTHING THAT'S IN HOLY BOOKS, even though THEY SAY THEY DO. They are afraid TO DISAGREE OUT LOUD.

Stop BEING ANNOYED at certain "FIGURES of SPEECH"; they do not HAVE TO MAKE LITERAL SENSE.

In THE SCIENCES, most EXPERTS AGREE about THE RULES; but in THE ARTS, they DO NOT.

The TRUE VALUE of ANYTHING is WHAT ANYONE is WILLING TO PAY.

THINGS that once were but are NO LONGER mostly SEEN as "SINS": Not going to church. WORKING on SUNDAY. SELLING on SUNDAY. "LIVING IN SIN," is no longer CONSIDERED A SIN by MOST PEOPLE.

We cannot ALL AGREE as to what should be A LAW or A SIN.

They are not REALLY LAWS or SINS, unless THE AUTHORITIES ENFORCE THEM and THE PEOPLE ABIDE BY THEM.

We are STUCK with HOLY BOOKS and ORGANIZED RELIGION, because THEY HAVE "PAINTED THEMSELVES INTO A CORNER."

There are ALWAYS a FEW on THE BOTTOM, who are JUST AS SMART or BRILLIANT, as MOST OF THOSE AT THE TOP.

Is anyone ALIVE ever BEYOND REDEMPTION?

The LOUD PERSON is the MOST DANGEROUS, but THE QUIET PERSON is apt to be THE MOST REASONABLE.

We cannot BE SURE of WHAT WE KNOW, until WE KNOW what WE DON'T KNOW.

If HALF of MARRIAGES end in DIVORCE, not all THOSE INTACT are HAPPY.

Is it A MISNOMER to CALL SEX, "MAKING LOVE?"

One of THE GREAT THINGS in LIFE is A VERY LOVING RELATIONSHIP with ANYONE.

Most people who ASK US FOR ADVICE, do not WANT THE TRUTH; they want us TO SAY SOMETHING to MAKE THEM FEEL BETTER.

It is ALWAYS WRONG to THINK that we are ALWAYS RIGHT.

Do you BELIEVE that THE KIND OF JUSTICE WE RECEIVE IN AMERICA depends on WHO WE ARE and HOW MUCH MONEY WE HAVE?

It is A PERSONAL FLAW or WEAKNESS, if we think WE HAVE NO PERSONAL FLAWS or WEAKNESSES.

EVERY NEW FRIEND WE MAKE will ultimately MAKE OUR LIVES BETTER or WORSE.

When WE DO NOT KNOW, we believe. When WE CANNOT BELIEVE, we guess. When WE CANNOT GUESS, we imagine. We can NEVER ADMIT NOT KNOWING or BEING IGNORANT.

There are physically SIGHTED PEOPLE who ARE "BLIND" and physically BLIND PEOPLE who have GREAT "VISION" or INSIGHT.

WE RESPECT STRENGTH – POSITIVE or NEGATIVE.

ORGANIZED RELIGION would "HAVE US BELIEVE" that all THE GREAT or BEST DECISIONS for OUR SPIRITUAL or MORAL LIVES were MADE 2000 YEARS AGO; when they did not KNOW WHAT A GERM WAS, or that THE EARTH WAS ROUND. They were not AS SMART as WE ARE TODAY.

We do not BELIEVE SOME THINGS WILL HAPPEN, until THEY HAPPEN.

Most people's FEELINGS ARE HURT, because THEY FEEL not LOVED, not LIKED or not RESPECTED.

We want to tell others HOW THEY SHOULD LIVE THEIR LIVES, but DON'T WANT THEM TELLING US.

We BLAME AUTHORITIES for NOT SOLVING CRIMES, as much AS WE BLAME CRIMINALS for COMMITTING THEM.

There is SOMETHING WRONG with people who are MOSTLY RIGHT, and SOMETHING RIGHT with people who are MOSTLY WRONG.

Our VICTORIES and SUCCESSES "SWELL OUR HEADS," and our FAULTS and FLAWS make us CRY.

There are some GREAT TALENTS that are not SUPERSTARS, and some SUPERSTARS that are not GREAT TALENTS.

Do you believe that THE HOLY BOOKS are THE WORDS OF GOD, the WORDS of ANCIENT RELIGIOUS LEADERS and SCRIBES, or THE WORDS of ANCIENT RELIGIOUS LEADERS who just WANTED TO CONTROL THE ILLITERATE MASSES?

The JOB DOES NOT ALWAYS MAKE PEOPLE HAPPY; HAPPY PEOPLE ALWAYS MAKE THE JOB HAPPY.

MOST OF US have A PROBLEM admitting THAT WE HAVE A PROBLEM.

RELATIVES that we have not SEEN IN DECADES always ASSUME that WE ARE THAT SAME PERSON THAT THEY ONCE KNEW.

Some people USE THEIR STRENGTHS in WEAK WAYS, and SOME PEOPLE use THEIR WEAKNESSES in STRONG WAYS.

If it is not a matter of FACTS, KNOWLEDGE or SCIENCE, it is just A MATTER OF OPINION.

Does REACHING "THE TOP" require MORE WORK, SKILL, and EDUCATION or MORE CRONYISM, NEPOTISM and LUCK?

What we MOST DEMAND from others, they tend to be LESS WILLING TO GIVE.

LOGIC is NEVER EMOTIONAL and EMOTION is RARELY LOGICAL.

FEELINGS never abide by ANY LAWS, and LAWS never consider any FEELINGS.

We must BE RECEPTIVE to LOVE in GENERAL, because WE CANNOT always DEMAND LOVE SPECIFICALLY.

Some of us ARE AFRAID of LIFE and DEATH.

We are SOCIAL ANIMALS; we cannot JUST "MIND OUR OWN BUSINESS."

We do not need A JUDGE or JURY to decide whom WE THINK are GUILTY.

GREAT ADVICE can USUALLY BENEFIT US. But RARELY can SAVE US.

MOST NEW LAWS are enacted TO PROTECT THE PUBLIC or TO PROTECT THE SENSIBILITIES of THE "LAWMAKERS."

IN THE PUBLIC ARENA, are WE PERSONS, or ARE WE JUST NUMBERS?

It is always "THE BEST OF TIMES" or "THE WORST OF TIMES" for SOMEONE.

SOME PARENTS try to LIVE THEIR CHILDRENS' LIVES FOR THEM.

Do you BELIEVE GOD can do things WITHOUT US or that GOD CAN ONLY DO THINGS THROUGH US?

We ESSENTIALLY GO THROUGH LIFE trying TO COMPENSATE for NOT BEING PERFECT.

In AMERICA, SOME LARGE CRIMES are "TOO BIG" to have been committed BY SINGLE PERSON, we always WANT TO BLAME SOMEONE ELSE TOO.

When more and more people MOVE OUT of a LARGE CITY, the POLICE RECEIVE CREDIT for "REDUCING CRIME."

Be SKEPTICAL of ANYONE who CLAIMS to HAVE "THE ULTIMATE ANSWER" or "THE FINAL SOLUTION" to ANYTHING.

There are GREAT PEOPLE who are WELL KNOWN, and GREAT PEOPLE who are UNKNOWN.

Some of us deal with OUR STRESS or EMBARRASSMENT, by CRYING, and some of us deal with it by SMILING or GIGGLING.

There is ALWAYS someone WHO ASPIRES TO BECOME, what WE ALREADY ARE.

OUR WORST can SPUR US to BECOME OUR BEST.

AFTER A WHILE, no one REMEMBERS who won THE PRESTIGIOUS AWARDS, except THOSE WHO WON THEM.

We are HAPPY about "THE UPSIDE" of SEX, and CRY about "THE DOWNSIDE."

EVERYTHING has A PRICE or A COST that cannot ALWAYS BE PAID WITH MONEY.

We cannot CONVINCE YOUNG PEOPLE that SOMETHING LIES BEYOND what they CAN SEE ON THE OUTSIDE.

There is something GOOD or BAD, and RIGHT or WRONG about EVERYONE – more or less.

When we are YOUNG, most of what WE KNOW or BELIEVE is SOMETHING someone HAS TOLD US or TAUGHT US.

Do not BE ASHAMED if you do not TREAT ALL OF YOUR CHILDREN THE SAME; we must ANSWER THE UNIQUE NEEDS of EACH CHILD.

Very few of us are GREAT PARENTS for the DURATION of OUR CHILDRENS' CHILDHOOD.

Amassing A FORTUNE will BENEFIT OTHERS more than it BENEFITS US.

We MUST ALWAYS ARGUE THAT WE ARE RIGHT, otherwise, WE MAY HAVE TO ADMIT THAT WE ARE WRONG, THAT SOMEONE ELSE is RIGHT, ADOPT A NEW PERSPECTIVE or CHANGE OUR LIVES.

Almost NOTHING, and NO ONE can be SCINTILLATING, INTERESTING, ENTERTAINING or AMUSING 24 hours a day, BUT TELEVISION TRIES.

We do not have to be RIGHT or CORRECT to IMPRESS PEOPLE.

If TELEVISION and OTHER MEDIA cannot RAISE PEOPLE to A HIGHER LEVEL, they are willing TO FOLLOW THEM DOWN to a LOWER LEVEL.

To some MEDIA CORPORATIONS only RATINGS and MONEY, MATTER.

Almost NONE OF US can ADMIT that we are TOO OLD to do ANYTHING.

If EVERYONE just CHANGED THEMSELVES, the WORLD WOULD BE CHANGED.

Some YOUNG PEOPLE do not STUDY THE PAST, because THEY BELIEVE that NOTHING IMPORTANT HAPPENED UNTIL AFTER THEY WERE BORN.

Some of us are NOT SMART ENOUGH to know HOW DUMB WE ARE.

If we are NOT QUALIFIED to HELP, our HELP CAN HARM.

Do you think of ALL CELEBRITIES as "REAL PEOPLE?"

Almost ALL CELEBRITIES are "ACTORS," more or less.

Some of us EXPECT TOO MUCH FROM GOD and NOT ENOUGH FROM OURSELVES.

We use DISTRACTIONS IN THE "OUTSIDE WORLD," to AVOID DEALING WITH OUR "INNER-SELVES."

We STILL THINK or BELIEVE that it is MORE ACCEPTABLE for MALES to monetarily provide FOR FEMALES, rather than FOR FEMALES to monetarily provide FOR MALES.

BLACK PEOPLE do not like to SEE ANY BLACK INDIVIDUALS behaving BADLY, because THEY KNOW that SOME WHITE PEOPLE will BLAME ALL BLACK PEOPLE.

It is not GLAMOROUS, to be expected ALWAYS to be GLAMOROUS.

It is NOT FUNNY to always need to be FUNNY.

We DO THINGS the way we DO THINGS, because that is the way WE HAVE ALWAYS DONE THINGS.

Most PEOPLE'S ADVICE to US is essentially, "YOU SHOULD BE MORE LIKE ME."

SCAM ARTISTS think ALL ELDERLY PEOPLE are RICH and GULLIBLE.

THE IRONY that NO ONE BELIEVES, is that some POOR PEOPLE are HAPPIER than some RICH PEOPLE.

We like ELDERLY PEOPLE who ACT YOUNG, because IT GIVES US HOPE.

It would BEHOOVE US to NOT BELIEVE EVERYTHING we have BEEN TOLD or TAUGHT.

Many, if not MOST OF US, do not ASK OURSELVES, how do we know WHAT WE KNOW, or WHY do we BELIEVE what WE BELIEVE?

We are NEVER SATISFIED with WHERE WE ARE, we always WANT TO MOVE TO THE NEXT LEVEL.

LUCK or "THE X FACTOR" is A PART of EVERY SITUATION, but it can NEVER BE PREDICTED or DEPENDED UPON.

The hardest people TO HELP are THOSE PEOPLE who WILL NOT HELP US to HELP THEM.

Some of us DO NOT DIFFERENTIATE between "HELPING PEOPLE" and TRYING to "SAVE PEOPLE."

There will ALWAYS BE PEOPLE WHO ARE NOT IN FAVOR of THEIR OWN GROWTH and EDUCATION: They do not want to be BIGGER, BETTER or BRIGHTER.

Some RELIGIONISTS, STREET PHILOSOPHERS and INTELLECTUALS are "MAKING UP" their FACTS or STATISTICS.

We are ALL trying TO CONVERT one another TO SEE, THINK, FEEL and BELIEVE the same as US.

Our lives ARE DOMINATED by MONEY, RELIGION, and THE DESIRE for POWER and SELF-GLORIFICATION.

SMALL MINDS think NOTHING is SOMETHING, or THAT SOMETHING is NOTHING.

Much of LIFE and THE WORLD are the WAY THEY ARE, we CANNOT ALWAYS CHANGE THEM; WE CAN ONLY ALWAYS CHANGE OURSELVES.

We cannot MAKE THE WORLD PERFECT; we can ONLY KEEP MAKING IT BETTER.

EVERYONE is DIFFERENT, but almost EVERYONE wants EVERYONE to BE THE SAME AS THEM. THINGS will NEVER BE as THEY ONCE WERE, NOR WILL they EVER BE EXACTLY as WE WISH THEY WERE.

HUMAN BEINGS are "WORKS IN PROGRESS"; we are still NOT FULLY ADULT, NOT FULLY HUMAN and NOT FULLY CIVILIZED.

We ALL LIVE OUR LIVES, CONTINUOUSLY SEARCHING FOR MONEY, LOVE and GOD, and SO DO ALL THE WORLDS' RELIGIONS.

A real question is, why does ORGANIZED RELIGION need SO MUCH or OUR MONEY – are they SELLING US GOD for A PRICE?

LOVE is CARING FOR OTHERS in THE SAME SENSE that WE CARE FOR OURSELVES.

Another way TO DEFINE GOD, is THE TOTAL or COLLECTIVE LOVE of EVERY PERSON.

LIFE is TOO COMPLEX or INTRICATE to be COMPLETELY or TOTALLY UNDERSTOOD or FIGURED OUT.

ULTIMATELY, we are NOT BEHOLDEN to RELIGION, MONEY, or THE PRESENT POWER STRUCTURE; WE are MOSTLY BEHOLDEN to "THE PREVAILING ZEITGEIST" and THAT IS ALWAYS CHANGING: What is WRONG TODAY, can be RIGHT TOMORROW, and WHAT IS "RIGHT CAN BE WRONG."

Made in the USA
Monee, IL
28 October 2024